Randomness

Randomness:
Short Stories & Poetry
You'll Never Be Bored With

By Sonia Gonzales

iUniverse, Inc.
New York   Bloomington

iUniverse books may be ordered through booksellers or by contacting:

iUniverse
1663 Liberty Drive
Bloomington, IN 47403
www.iuniverse.com
1-800-Authors (1-800-288-4677)

Because of the dynamic nature of the Internet, any Web addresses or links contained in this book may have changed since publication and may no longer be valid. The views expressed in this work are solely those of the author and do not necessarily reflect the views of the publisher, and the publisher hereby disclaims any responsibility for them.

ISBN: 978-1-4401-8827-5 (sc)
ISBN: 978-1-4401-8829-9 (hc)
ISBN: 978-1-4401-8829-9 (ebook)

Printed in the United States of America

iUniverse rev. date: 12-23-09

This book would not be possible without my family, my JasnNCarly fans, and my friends. To all of you, I give my endless thanks and respect. You know who you are.

I dedicate this book to my angel in heaven, my biggest cheerleader of all time, my daddy…Richard Eugene Rue. I miss you more than words could ever express. No matter where life takes me, I will always be your little princess. A piece of me is always with you. I love you, Mama, and David in this life as well as beyond.

To Liz, Kali, Monda, McCarly, and my P.I.C. Myself 18 – you are the most amazing, supportive women. I am a blessed writer and individual to constantly have you kicking me into gear.

Lastly, Mama, I want you to know that your support and love means the world to me. If I don't say it enough, please know how much I appreciate your strength and love. You are the best mother and friend a girl at any age could ask for.

To the Reader,

This book is a collection written from an early age up until now. I picked the poems and stories I felt most connected to and placed them in this book. I wanted to show the progression in my creative writing as it is the only form I have not been able to share until now.

In this book, you will find dates attached to many titles. The date signifies when the story or poem had begun. My father taught me poetry at the age of nine and helped me develop story ideas soon after. However, in many of my stories, you will see how everyone has been a heavy influence on my writing and my perspective.

I decided to share this book, despite all fear of failure and perfection, because of my current readers. They have been urging me to go beyond what I share and reveal my purest creative mind. To them, I hope it was worth the wait. To you, I hope you connect to the different characters and situations exploding off the following pages.

Contents

Bonds For Life

Lazy Love

Real World Worries

Womanly Wiles

Bonds For Life

Entitlement (2002)

B and I were good friends until the day he challenged my throne.

I was about six when it happened.

A large collection of the shorty population in the complex rounded up to play a game of hide and seek.

We were taking a break from the game and drinking kool-aid.

B felt it was his duty to finally break the news to me.

The news being that I was not a princess.

"Yes, I am."

"No you're not."

"Yes, I am."

"Prove it!"

"Fine!" I shouted before stomping up towards my apartment.

I led B and our friend towards my apartment, hurt my friend did not take me on my word.

I knocked on the door, figuring it would be less trouble than going up to Mom for confirmation.

"She's coming!" One of the kids said, watching my mom leaving the kitchen through our sliding glass door.

Mom's surprise was obvious as she opened the door to us.

All of us looked up at her with different appearances. Our friends were looking up at her with smiles and their hands behind their backs, playing the role of well behaved children. B stood there with a sigh, looking as though I was telling on him.

"Yes?" My mom said, unsure of why she had a parade of little people at her door.

B spoke up, "Tell her she's not a princess."

Mom smiled, letting out a small laugh, and shook her head, "But she is. She's her daddy's little princess."

"See, I told you!" I snapped, placing my hands on my hips and sticking my tongue out.

I let my ponytail give B my final 'hmph' before going into my apartment.

Needless to say, the princess sat proudly on her throne for the remainder of the day.

Girlfriend (A Memoir Tribute to Grade School Love)

"Sonia, why don't you go outside? Make some new friends." Daddy urged while sitting in his wheel chair and watching the television.

"Nah." I responded while continuing to write in my poetry book.

Mama and Daddy exchanged worried looks. We had just moved into the trailer park, and I rarely strayed out of the house. They had planned to move before the new school year in order for me and David to make some new friends. But it still bugged me. I had finally fit in with a group at my old school, and I had to start the fifth grade as one of the in crowd. Of course, my parents had to yank it away from me. My one chance to be someone special, and I would not have the chance to do it. Latasha, Cassandra, and all my other friends would be moving on without me. Great, on top of everything else I can tell everyone I lived in a trailer park.

There was one nice thing about the place. It was ours. The trailer was a little old and a bit of fixer upper, but it was ours. Finally, our own place.

Daddy sat there as long as he could, encouraging me to go outside and 'play', and Mama watched with patience. He sat as long as he could before retiring back to the bedroom. That's when it happened. I was in my room, listening sadly to my Mama encouraging my brother, "My friends are my friends, Mom. She can find her own."

Mama continued, "Ay, David, she could use some help. Just introduce her to a couple of friends then she can find her own."

"Why can't she just go hang out with that girl Samantha across the street?"

"No, that little witch is nothing but trouble. I'd rather Sonia lock herself in her room than hang out with that little gringa."

"So be it."

"David Eugene Rue, you better help your sister out or I'm going to make sure the only friends you have are the bucket of army men in your closet. Comprehende?"

"Fine!"

How pathetic was I? I had to have my stupid little brother help me? If any of my girls found out about this, I would never hear the end of it. I grabbed my pen and journal. I had to get out of the room and out of the house before David dragged his buck toothed friends, to laugh at me.

I found a pretty nice tree on the corner of our street and sat beneath it. Once I started writing, I realized I was making a diary entry rather than writing another poem. I talked about missing the dark apartment we lived in, about missing my friends, and most of all missing the benefits of being known. I had to start all over again, and I didn't want to especially in the trailer park. I scribbled on the paper relentlessly until I was overcome by a shadow darker than the shade of the tree. I knew it was David, and I spotted the pair of sneakers beside him. I closed my eyes, afraid to see what I was about to be exposed to, as David's voice filled the air, "I've been looking for you."

"Yea, well, you found me." I huffed, opening my eyes only to look at my writing.

"I want you to meet my friend." David sighed, "Raymond this is my sister. Sonia, this is Raymond."

Finally, I looked up. He was not a complete nerd, but he was still a boy. This meant our immediate disliking of each other. The last guy I had tolerated was Frankie, and he irritated me easily. Raymond was about my height, dark, and he had little ears that stuck out slightly. I had to bow my head to keep from laughing, but I couldn't contain my smile.

David sensed the meeting was over, "Okay, I'm gonna go get that sandwich mom promised me. You coming?"

Raymond's voice filled the air for the first time, "I'll wait for you."

I heard David's voice get lower, "Sorry, man, I'll be quick."

He whispered causing me to angrily squint my eyes.

"He eats a lot, doesn't he?" Raymond asked.

"Pretty much." I simply told him. I wish David had took his dork of friend. I wanted to be alone. I didn't want to be alone with David's reject.

So what if he looked pretty normal? There had to be something wrong with him, if he was hanging out with my little brother. I was going to continue with my writing when Raymond knelt down and interrupted me, "So, what are you writing?"

"None of your business." I snapped.

"Whatever. Are you any good?"

I frowned, meeting his eyes with mine, "Any good?"

"At writing?"

"What do you care?"

Nothing came out of his mouth for a few seconds, and I started to feel self-conscience.

He sat, facing me, and examined me with his eyes. I hated this. I hated being stared at. When he finally spoke again, I was more than surprised by his comment, "You're mean."

"No, I'm not."

"Yea, you are." Raymond insisted, causing me to roll my eyes, "What's your problem?"

"Why is it your business?"

"Fine, forget I asked." He gave up, throwing his hands up in surrender.

A long silence fell between us, and all I could think was, Where the hell is David? Raymond was not going anywhere. He just sat there, staring at me. I felt the urge to continue our conversation, "I'm not mean."

"You are to me."

"You don't even know me."

He looked at me with a bit of an irritated look, "Whose fault's that?"

Unfortunately, he was right. I hated to admit it, and I didn't... aloud. I closed my journal and decided to try, "What grade are you in?"

"I should tell you it's none of your business." Raymond snapped, making me regret my decision," But I'm gonna be in fifth." He said and offered me a small smile. That was how we met, and it was probably the most eventful thing to happen to me all summer.

Raymond did make it easier to meet new people. I had made a pretty good circle of friends before we started fifth grade. This made it easier to make friends in school. But the more friends I made, the less time and the less effort I put into my friendship with Raymond. Besides, I was going out with somebody. This meant I circled yes on a piece of paper, and I was officially someone's girlfriend. Never mind that I barely talked to the guy.

Once David told me Raymond knew about my boyfriend, I began to notice Raymond wasn't talking to me much. It was weird, but I got over it. Then came the day when I was sick of James. When James was out of the picture, Raymond started hanging out again.

It was back to normal.

Until the day I started noticing some guys laughing at me. I paid no attention to it until my friend, Bonnie, came to me and explained what was going on, "James told everyone about you two."

I laughed, "What about us?"

"He told everybody you were..." Bonnie was as cautious as possible, "Easy." How could I be easy? He kissed my cheek, and that was it. I accepted the laughs painfully and made it through the end of my day.

There I locked myself in my room. I wasn't even to Jr. High, and I was already easy. My dad, mom, and David made trips to my door, but I wanted to be alone. It was close to dinnertime when David knocked on my door. I told him to go away, but he told me, "Raymond wants to talk you."

After I wiped my eyes, I opened my door. I headed to the door and wondered if Raymond would tell me exactly what James said. I opened the door to find Raymond waiting. I closed the door and immediately looked anywhere but at Raymond's concerned eyes. I didn't have to wait long before he broke the silence, "What happened?"

"You didn't hear?" This surprised me. I had assumed all of fifth grade knew.

"No. David just said you were crying." Raymond shoved his hands into his pockets nervously, "Are you okay?"

"No." I snapped, feeling the tears refuel, "James told everyone I was easy."

Raymond couldn't help but laugh, "Easy? You?"

"It's not funny."

He quickly got serious again, "Sorry." Raymond remained silent for a minute before letting out a long breath, "Are you gonna kick his ass tomorrow?"

Raymond knew me way too well. I smiled, trying to find the humor in this, "I want to. But Bonnie says it only makes me look worse." I shook my head, wondering how I got myself into this, "I'm supposed to ignore it or laugh it off or something like that."

"Oh." Was all he could say. I was going to go back in when Raymond stopped me, "Do you want me to fix it?"

I turned to him confused, "What?"

"I could fix it. Tomorrow." Raymond insisted, "Do you want me to?"

I wasn't sure what he meant, "What are you going to do?"

"Just say yes or no." Raymond instructed, causing me to nod yes. He grinned, beginning to descend the stairs, telling me, "Stop crying. I'll fix it tomorrow."

The next day, I was a basket of nerves. Raymond, David, and I squeezed into a seat in the back of the bus. I looked past Raymond's stone expression to see David's goofy grin. It was suddenly so clear.

I punched Raymond's arm, "You told him, didn't you?"

"What's it matter?" He snapped, rubbing his arm.

"You haven't told me what's going on, but you told him?"

"Would you just chill?" He noticed my look, "He's got my back, that's it."

"Your back?" I questioned with disbelief, "I can take him in ten seconds."

Raymond ignored my last comment and stared straight once again. I knew what he was going to do. And it was instantaneous when we got off the bus. James was running late as usual and getting on the grounds right when we got there. Raymond took off in spite of my plea, "Raymond, don't."

Poor James, he never saw it coming. Raymond had tackled him to the ground and started throwing punches before James even saw his face. I ran to the circle of urging kids and shoved my way to the two. I felt a little sorry when I found Raymond on the ground, straddling James, and James' friends who laughed. I felt a little sorry, but I didn't stop it either.

Raymond stopped hitting him to grab his collar and shout in his face, "Take it back!"

James was confused, "What back?"

What back? I couldn't believe he acted like he had done nothing to me.

"Take back what you said about my girlfriend." Raymond demanded, winding his fist back, clearly warning James to be quick.

James looked fearfully at Raymond's knuckles, "Okay! Okay! I lied!"

Just after the confession, the teacher appeared. Raymond was yanked off James by the collar of his coat. The teacher held him secure while James moved on the ground, "Who started this?"

"He did." Raymond snapped before his smile appeared, "I just finished it." The teacher sighed, shaking his head, "Let's go."

Raymond didn't have much of a chance to protest as he was carried by his collar to the principal's office, looking like a puppy dog being picked up by the roll of his neck.

The circle dissolved, and I was left to David, James, and the three cronies that thought James was a hero before this morning. James looked at me both angry and apologetic.

I had to get away, "Come on, Dave." I urged, tugging at David's bulky sleeve.

"Just a sec." David agreed before using all his might to kick James while he was on the ground, "Don't mess with my sister!"

It was true. Raymond had fixed everything with James. James tried to lie again all day, but who was going to believe him now? However, by fixing my problem, Raymond created another.

Now, in this episode of my fifth grade life, I had a bully boyfriend.

The whole situation was new to me. I had never been the damsel in distress, and I usually had no problem sticking up for myself. But I felt helpless this time, and a boy who was my close friend had to take care of it. I didn't know why, and I was dying to ask him. I hadn't seen him all day and the rumors ran rapid.

"I heard he made James cry."

"I heard he knocked out his tooth."

"I heard the principal spanked him."

"Yeah, right before he got kicked outta school."

It was hard to concentrate. I explained to Mama what happened, and she immediately volunteered to make my favorite dinner. So while me and David did homework in the kitchen, Mama was on the other side frying cheeseburgers and baking trench fries.

Suddenly, there was a knock at the front door.

David was quick to stand, but Mama's look sat him back down. She flipped the burgers and went to the door. I knew who it was when Mama grinned in amusement. She was loud when announcing him, "Sonia! Tyson's here."

I gave her the dirtiest look possible and headed for the door. Mama winked at me as we passed each other, and I wanted to scream. Raymond waited with a nervous smile. He didn't have a scratch on him, so he was fully aware I told Mama what happened.

"Hey" was all we could say to each other at first. We silently sat on the porch steps and tried to figure out how to start.

"Did you really get kicked out?" I asked cautiously, because I knew if it was true his mom was going to kill him.

"No, but my mom had to pick me up. The principal said I needed to," He temporarily impersonated our principal, "Cool off."

"I'm sorry."

"Don't worry about it. I wanted to do it." I frowned, "Why?"

Raymond shrugged, looking towards his feet, "I don't like seeing you cry." I could understand that. I probably wouldn't like seeing him cry either. It took a minute for me to get the courage to ask what I had been wondering all day, "Why did you say it?"

"Say what?"

"You know what?"

Raymond took his time to answer me, and I was reminded why boys irritated me. He looked over at me with a dismissive look, "You're a girl, right?" I nodded.

"And you're my friend?" I nodded.

"So you're my girlfriend." He concluded before looking away.

It took me a minute to process, "Don't pull that crap with me. I just wanna know why."

Raymond was annoyed, "Because you were my girlfriend before you met him. He just gave you a stupid note before me."

"But you didn't say anything." I responded, wondering when this was understood.

"I didn't think I had to."

"But I didn't know." I snapped causing him to huff angrily. I let him simmer in his anger while I crossed my arms.

Raymond interrupted our silence, "Well, you know you're my girlfriend now, right?"

I didn't know how to react. Raymond was my best friend, and I didn't want to be anyone's girlfriend anymore. But I owed him, and I did, kinda, like him, "Yeah, I know now."

"Good." Raymond said with one last huff.

There was long period where we sat on the porch, officially boyfriend and girlfriend now. It seemed somewhat comfortable until I felt his arm wrapped around me.

I was quick to react, "Don't touch me, Raymond." I ordered, and his arm was gone. It was awkward for another period of time until I looked over at him and smiled. His smile back assured me nothing really had to change.

Our Angel, Analecia (2003)

There's an angel on her way,
With her presence comes a new and hopeful day,
We know her only through fuzzy photographs,
But somehow we can see her smile and hear her laugh.

She's already got a shirt reading princess and loving gifts piled
toward the sky,
Every time her mother speaks of her – you see that certain twinkle
in her eye,
Her father's still growing up but she's already his greatest
accomplishment,
Speaks of her when he can without giving his fear a hint.

To a mother whose children are rapidly learning to fly their own
way,
This little bundle of joy gives her chance to put her silliness on
display,
To me she's the miracle we didn't know we wanted,
Didn't know our lives were individually haunted.

This little life was not planned but she will never lack love,
For we all know (whatever the reason) she's a gift from above,
Pretty soon, I'll be Auntie Sonia and I can't wait,
Out little Angel Ana will truly be something great.

What I Can't Do (2002)

I want to say thank you,
But the right words won't appear,
Because no matter what I say,
You're no longer here,
I want to say I love you,
But no words could ever express,
Your power solely,
To bring me absolute happiness.

You left an ache,
Where your presence resided,
You left a pain,
Since you left – it hasn't subsided,
You made me believe in perfection,
Before he decided it was your time,
You showed me beauty,
Leaving only a memory behind.

I miss hearing your heartbeat,
Assuring me you're here,
I miss your bear hugs,
And knowing you're near,
I miss your eyes,
Where I found home,
I miss your smile,
I hate feeling this alone.

I keep hoping this is a cruel joke,
Hoping you'll remind me how to laugh and simply be,
Now, all I can do is choke,
Because missing you means I can't breathe…

I hate needing anyone but you,
I am in so much pain and don't know what to do,
I hate clinging to others,
When I know you're the only one who wanted me to,
I can't begin to explain how I need you.

miss holding your hand,
Miss hearing you call me crazy,
Why did it have to end,
Your absence still amazes me.

I wish my wishes could bring you here,
I wish I could lose all my fear,
How will I live without you and all myself,
How do I exist without your help?

I have to believe you're in a better place or I'll lose my mind,
I have to believe there's a smile on your face – I'm just waiting for
a sign,
I hate waiting to dream to spend time with you,
I hate wanting to scream because we're no longer two.

I wanted to save you,
But that power wasn't mine,
I wanted to be with you,
But it's not my time,
Daddy, I live to make you proud.

Dads and Brothers (2002)

I loved my Daddy so much that it was hard to share him
Especially when my brother began to join me in my late night
journey
Two children crawling out of bed and sneaking off to observe the
wise one.

We would watch him in awe, peaking into the room with wide eyes
and gaping jaws
There he was, trying to contain his manly laughing at Letterman
My brother was stunned, "I still don't get it!"
I would shoot him a dirty look to quiet down, "Get what?"
"How can he be so big and still cry after he gives us a spankin'?"
"It's because you're evil, and he knows he can't whoop it outta
ya."

Though I despised my brother's intrusion, always in the way
I had to share my daddy, in every journey throughout my childhood
Evil Brothers...they always get in the way

Grandma Gonzales (2002)

"All right, you two, we just ate"
a Mother's warning into the backseat, typical of weekend visit
quickly following up her words with a look, saying
You act like angels all you want,
But I can see your horns.

When we finally parked,
the rules were completed with her last bit of frustration,
"When Grandma asks you if you're hungry, you're full!"
It seemed like an easy task for me and baby bro,
we were far from starving.

However, our efforts were futile
as the smell of spices, green bananas, bacalow,
pasteles, and so much more
You'd think Grandma was answering Mama's challenge,
daring us and encouraging us to behave badly.

Our stomach, being the demon is was,
spoke for us when Grandma asked,
"Are you hungry?"
We had to comply with nods,
sending our Grandma's angry squint at our parents.
How dare they not feed the kids?

The Gift (A Memoir about Mama)

My fourteenth birthday was right around the corner, and I didn't know what I wanted. Maybe, I really wanted to be powerful with tons of money and magic wand which made everyone I disliked disappear. I had nothing normal. I was a loner. I was a Latina who loved school and still thought boys were yucky. I tried to fit in, but it never worked out. When I tried to be "Latin," it was not enough. I had the look but not the accent for my friends. I was somehow trying to be black, if there was more than one 'dark' girl I hung out with. Never pretty enough to hang out with the popular girls, I hated the makeup they tried to make me wear. Lastly, if I tried to be one of the guys, I was lesbiana. It was painfully obvious, I just didn't fit in. My Daddy was my best friend, my Mama my drill sergeant, and my brother my annoyance. Nope, no one understood.

The only outlet I had was my Monday night, when Buffy the Vampire Slayer made me feel strangely normal. At the time, I felt alone because Daddy couldn't always perk me up like a cappuccino for a caffeine addict in the morning. I needed something more, and I didn't have to fit in with anyone when I had Buffy. In a weird way, I could relate the issues on the shows and was happy to watch the characters deal with issues beneath the demon surface. I even thought it would be cool if the demons at my school had the appearances of the ones Buffy had to slay. On the show, no one meant more to me than the Queen Nerd. Willow Rosenberg was the meek, weak, computer geek who played sidekick to Buffy and pined for Xander. She was me minus the cute best friend part. Strong inside yet too weak externally, she expressed it only in beautiful moments. For the most part, she just made it so I didn't always feel alone.

One day, I came home to find Mama with a ridiculously big smile on her face.

Immediately, I was suspicious. Mama smiling? Did we win the lottery?

Daddy called me into the room, and I entered to find the two of them. I presented a smile and brace the storm, "Yea?"

Now, it wasn't that Mama was typically unhappy, or that she never smiled, but today Mama was overjoyed. That I rarely saw. It was like she had found a cure for the common cold or that headache she was always getting.

I waited while Daddy nodded to her, "Well, what's going on?"

"I've gotta a surprise for you." Mama beamed while Daddy looked away, trying not to steal her thunder.

I knew something was up. Something was being hidden from me, "What?"

"Well, that all depends, do you want your birthday present now or in September?"

I assumed the big joke was what she was hiding behind her back. It had me confused. I knew she had something, but what was it? I tried to stand up on my tip toes being the short, big girl that I was, and found nothing.

Mama was good, not even a peek.

It had to be a trick. Why would I be getting my gift early? But I took a fool's way in and complied as any other fourteen-year-old given this choice: "Now."

"Well, I can show it to you not, but you'll still get it in September." Mama nudged Daddy as she handed me the paper in her hand.

Disappointed, I took it. This was great. I wouldn't even have a gift on my birthday in August? What a joke! I sighed and looked at the pamphlet in front of me. I still didn't get it. I glanced at the advertisement for a Sci-Fi weekend that was to take place in Denver with big star guests. Like I cared.

I frowned, "A Trekie convention?"

"Look inside!" Mama said with the patience of a girl my age.

I did as told, like always, and found a bigger advertisement before me. The event would include games based on different shows, auctions and booth sales, and guest speakers. I was paying attention until I saw exactly who would be there. It was her. It was Willow.

I felt like crying, jumping, screaming, any and everything I could think of. That was until I saw the price. We had recently moved into our new home and, though the convention was only a hundred for both of us, it was still a hundred I was sure we could not afford.

I looked at Mama and Daddy, trying not to get my hopes up, "We're going?"

Mama laughed at the question, "Why would I show that to you, if we weren't?"

Who was I to question her? She was completely right. If she had the money, who was I to steal her thunder?

A smile spread across my face from ear to ear as I felt tears forming. I was going to meet Willow. Alyson Hannigan, my hero, would be my birthday gift.

~*~

After a day of torture, we had finally made it to Denver and settled in our hotel. Once we had our things put away, we walked over to the hotel where the convention was actually being held. As we did, my reservations rang through my ears. I was a heavy girl, and I never felt good in crowds. I was Puerto Rican and, for some reason, I didn't think that would be widely received at a Sci-Fi convention.

As we entered the doors, immediately, any fears I had were gone. There were tons of people and, oddly enough, they were all weird. I finally found a place where I felt a little more comfortable being myself.

We made our way to the line to get our may, lay out of events, and dates for guest speakers. Thank God Mom was there because I wasn't listening at all. I was looking at the huge hotel connected to the center and looking at people around me. I work one of my Buffy shirts to show my support, my reason for being there. I was nowhere near decked out like some people who were in full Trekie get up. Kling ons, blue aliens, Captain Kirks, and Spocks filled the place. Everywhere you looked there was something new to be in awe of.

Mama brought me out of my daze, asking if I wanted to go to the purchasing room. I wasn't so sure. I would be meeting Willow tomorrow, and what if she was selling something? I had been working at a summer job and put together $100, but I didn't want to blow it right away.

"Nah, I can wait. I don't want to spend all my money."

Mama shrugged my comment off, "Don't worry, we have plenty of money. It's your birthday, have fun."

"My birthday was in August." I said it without thinking, and Mama wasn't mad. For that, I silently thanked God and admitted I owed him one.

"Come on." Mama insisted and led me into the huge room without any pressure.

It was full of every little gidget, gadget, picture, poster, figure, doll, and lunchbox you could think of. God, where could I begin? I wanted to be cautious, but everything was there. First, I had to get a picture for Willow to sign, something a little classier than the collage I had made. Then, there was a magazine for her to sign. Oh, and they had pictures of the whole cast. Tons and tons of pictures. Oh, and the postcards, and playing cards...well..you get the idea.

~*~

That night, I couldn't sleep. It wasn't only because of my excitement or Mama's snoring.

I had struggled with something all day.

I turned to face my Mama in the bed next to me and continued to be puzzled.

She lied flat on her back, her mouth ajar, and her eyes shut. If it wasn't for her loud snarl, I wouldn't know she was alive.

Mama and I were not nearly as close me and Daddy. So I did not understand why she would go through so much trouble to make this happen for me. All day she wore that smile, constantly remind me that I would meet my hero tomorrow, and it bothered me a little. Sure, she tried to take me to the mall, tried to watch Buffy with me, even tried to listen to my music. But she didn't understand me or get my feelings.

She couldn't possibly understand what it felt like to be punished for being smart, punished for being way overweight, for not liking what the other girls did. Why was she trying? She wouldn't get it.

But she was. She continued to try to understand, regardless of how many times she had failed.

Then, I painfully asked myself why she would do something so nice for someone who tried so hard to shut her out?

I couldn't sleep. I got out of bed and walked over to the window.

Today had been the most time Mama had spent with me in so long. Today mom...was Mama.

I crossed my arms, holding in tears, and watched the stray cars on the highway. I can't tell you how long I had stood there before I heard Mama's voice, "Sonia?"

"Hmm?" I wiped away any stray tears before facing her, continuing to bow my head.

"You better get some rest, small fry. You don't want to be yawning when you meet Willow." Flashing me a drowsy grin, Mama instantly fell back into a deep slumber.

I felt the tears refuel as I realized she had called me small fry. Something she had not called me in years.

~*~

The next morning we left to the center early because although we knew she'd be there that day, we didn't know what time. We lined up at ten 'o clock in the morning behind a few people. I was sure to count. We were tenth. Mama and I stood, realizing the lines were forming around us.

Mama was quick to say, "It's gonna be a long day."

We waited for about an hour before the hours were posted for each star. Willow wouldn't be there until "around" one thirty.

I nodded happily, beginning my countdown, before I sat down right where I had lined up.

Mama was already seated, telling me she'd keep my place while I checked the time.

When I returned, Mama volunteered, "Do you want to go check out something else and come back later?"

"No, I'm gonna stay in line." I stubbornly stated, knowing in my gut that line would be out the door. Sitting with my goody bag, I stared straight ahead of me.

Mama laughed, shaking her head, and remained silent.

I dared people with my look. Cut in front of me, see what happens. I warned people with my posture, I wasn't messing around. This was happening for me, and I'd be damned if anyone prevented it.

Hours passed, and Mama continued to make suggestions. She would stay in line as I waited, things of that nature. But I wouldn't budge.

When it was one thirty on the dot, Willow was nowhere to be found.

"There she is!"

With the statement, I managed a glimpse at her red mane between all the bodies. I felt the excitement mix with nerves and tears. Indeed, it was her.

It was my hero right before my eyes.

Mama suddenly went into bodyguard mode, "She better be as nice as her character. Because if she's a little prim donna, I'm gonna give her a piece of my mind."

I rolled my eyes and gave her a look, "Not Willow, Mama."

"She better not." Mama smoother my hair, tugged my shirt, and stated, "Nobody hurts my baby."

I bowed my head, turning straight.

I had been hurt. That's why I was so happy to be here. Everyone at school hurt me. Every time I didn't fit in, it hurt me. Mama's time with me or lack thereof hurt me. But not Willow.

She would never do such a thing. She made me fit.

We started to get closer, and my stomach was tying in knots. I began to notice, in pieces offered to me through glances, her wide smile, her kind eyes, and...she cut her hair!

I felt everything overwhelming me. My Daddy had joked that I not trip or ask her if she wanted a beer (a mishap he had with Chuck Berry).

Terrified, I wondered what if she doesn't like me. But she had to. She was like me, and she would understand.

I waited while my hands shook, palms sweated. Nervous because the woman I put on a pedestal was about to meet her biggest fan.

I had in my bag a collector's magazine of a Buffy issue for her to sign and a collage I had made. With a collection of pictures from the internet, I had learned very interesting facts like how she liked Roy Jetson because she loved all of his toys.

My heartbeat got irregular, and I realized we were up.

My fear was gone when I saw Alyson Hannigan welcome me with a wide grin.

All I could think was I can't believe it's her. A woman I watch every week go through my life with the same uncertainty. She had been my voice since the first episode, and I even had a tribute screen name to her, WillowKix.

I slowly approached and, surprisingly, I didn't trip. However, I did manage to blurt out, "My heart is beating so fast."

What an idiot. Like Willow cared about my heartbeat. Such a dork.

She smiled and giggled, "Oh, it's ok."

Then she gave me a hug, and I knew she was as cool as the expectations I had set.

I continued with ease, "Ok first things first, I wanted to give you this."

Handing her a letter I had written, I accompanied it with a beanie bag owl to add to her collection.

"And I was wondering if you could sign these for me--to Sonia?"

I don't remember if I took a breath or not, but I wanted to get it out and say everything before I lost my nerve.

She nodded, cheery the whole time, "Sure." Her eyes widened as I placed the collage before her, gasping, "This is so neat." Alyson told me and pointed quickly to a picture she had taken when she was little, "Oh my God, where did you get this?! Is this on the net? Geez, I don't even remember how old I was."

As she signed, I nodded, "Yea, it's on the net."

After she was done, she handed it back to me, "There you go."

Then I quickly added, "Oh and can I get a picture?"

She smiled up at me and nodded again, "Sure."

At this time, I don't think any of it was hitting me completely. As Mama took the picture, I finally remembered her presence. She was glowing, just as I was.

Alyson gave me one last hug before Mama went to her, handing her the collectible magazine and asking, "Can you sign this?"

"Who is this to?" She asked, watching Mama turn to me.

"WillowKix?" Mama asked me and I, still dazed, finally nodded. Seeing Alyson's confused look, Mama explained the name, "It's her screen name."

Alyson smiled at me again, appreciative, then jotted her signature, "Cool."

I was again in shock that Alyson thought I was cool and, reluctantly, left my hero to return to my everyday life.

Mama had to call after me so I would stop at the desk just outside the meeting room. It then hit me, and I burst into tears.

Willow was everything I expected and so much more.

Mama could only laugh as I repeatedly said, "She was so nice." Nothing more. Nothing less.

Once outside of the building, Mama lit up a cigarette and sat on the curb with me.

I knew she was watching as all my nerves let loose.

When I had calmed down a little, Mama asked a question that was so easily answered by my tears, "So...happy birthday?"

I looked at Mama, noticing her mixture of sadness and happiness. And though I had met my hero today, it would be a little fact in comparison to all the trouble Mama had gone through to get me here: the money she spent, the headaches she suffered, the smile she wore for two days. She made this happen.

Nodding slowly, I hugged her tightly.

Maybe the real hero was the woman who made the bus magically appear just when I thought we'd never get to the convention. Maybe the hero was the woman who bought those gifts for my memories. Maybe the hero was the woman who gave me the gift I would always remember...the one I had always wanted...a little understanding.

Moments of Possibility (2002-2009)

A short diary entry in a red covered, multicolored page book
became three pages poems
which turned into long fan fiction stories for actual fan response

The girl who wrote those things went from her life as Sony
to her life as WillowKix,
meeting her hero at 14 due to her mother's finesse
to her life as JasnNCarly,
who made friends for life through a bond in fictional wants buried
by soap writers' ignorance
to her life as LafayetteNTara,
who saw one woman's humor and imagination rejuvenate interest
among adults
- reacting with childlike enthusiasm for a adult encounters between
Vampires and all magic creatures
to a life which eventually brought her back to Sonia,
who met her hero John beyond HBO and was encourage to follow
her dreams

All the possibilities were confronting the little girl within,
she retreated further and further into herself
Until Mama finally pulled her aside,
telling her the adult she had become was ready to share it all
damn the consequences
It was her who gave the girl life
and the much need last piece, her biggest moment of possibility

Lazy Love

My Love (2001)

I don't think love for me has ever appeared,
Because if it had – it would still be here,
For the man I love is too strong to let me get away,
The man I love is too strong to let me run astray,
The man I love will hold me close when all I want to do is cry,
The man I love will give me a reason to live when I want to die,
The man I love is pure and true,
His soul shines through and through,
The man I love is perfect perhaps only in the eyes of mine,
The man I love is so much more than dollars and a dime,
The man I love is calm and talks to me,
Knows when I don't understand – he can make me see,
The man I love can please me more than physically,
He touches my soul and brings out the best emotionally,
The man I love his age is timeless,
He wonders open minded yet not mindless,
The man I love listens even when I'm yelling,
He smiles and absorbs my dreams and storytelling,
The man I love is protective but in no way overbearing,
The man I love is kind and caring,
The man I love can make me laugh when I don't feel I can take a joke,
His smile gives me breath when I feel like I can only choke,
The man I love knows each and every one of my fears,
He uses the softest of kisses to remove my tears,
To you this man I love may seem nothing more than a human being,
But to me he is so much more than that…he is my everything.

Untamable Heart (2003)

You want me to be your woman then be my man,
To keep me by your side – just hold my hand,
Try to confine me and lose,
Control or happiness – you have to choose,
I don't want to possess you but I want to know you're mine,
Need you to remind me of what we have from time to time.

Don't ignore me when you're with your boys,
They may not mind but I do,
You could use them like toys,
But I'm who you come home to.

If you lose me, you'll lose the best thing,
Miss out on all good love can bring,
You often neglect me,
Forgetting to respect me,
Asking me to keep my cool,
While playing your fool,
Talking to everything in heels,
Searching for something real,
Tossing them thousands of smiles,
I'm at home waiting all the while.

And I won't deny the beat of my heart with a look into your eyes,
Or how your touch awakens my stomach's butterflies,
But you're now ignoring how I was caught,
When your words meant more than what you bought.

I want to leave but again you block the door,
Still claiming I'm your want and nothing more,
But I've been feeling nothing like what you adore,
I feel nothing but pain at my core.

That's why I'll leave…one day,
Because I can't always live this way.

Every Little Thing

"It's just bread, Erica. It's not that big of a deal."

"It is a big deal. You can't always get what's on sale, all right? Sometimes it's just worth an extra buck."

If that's the case, big balla, why not just make it from scratch?

He managed to keep the thought to himself, shoving the loaf back on the shelf and grabbing the one she had requested. Shooting her a quick glare, he carefully laid it in the basket of the shopping cart and signaled for her to proceed.

"I love you."

So you say.

He looked away from her entirely, trying to focus on the busy atmosphere around them, but his eyes drifted back to her as she escaped one aisle only to submerge herself in the very next one. Unable to contain himself, he caught up to her quickly, "Don't you have a list?"

"Yes, but there's a sale on some stuff."

Just not the bread, right?

He pressed on, "Isn't the point of a list to avoid hours in the grocery story?"

"If we do this now, we don't have to come back."

Rolling his eyes, he let out a heavy sigh and shoved his hands in his pockets.

Dear Lord, please give me patience. Please, help me be content in this. Please help me love her.

~*~

I'm just trying to save you some damn money and time! Do you have to bitch about everything John? Keep fucking with me, and I will be praying for forgiveness for what I did to you with my lab book! It's not like I'm too happy about our quality time right now either.

Rather than say this, she retrieved a can of soup from the shelf and pretended to focus on the label.

I can't do this anymore. One more second of this, and this boy is going to be in that heavenly kingdom he's suddenly become so found of.

She glanced towards her boyfriend, briefly contemplating chucking the can at his head before returning it to its spot. Turning to him completely, frustrated by his irritated look, she crossed her arms and conceded, "Fine, let's just finish the list and go."

"Are you sure?"

Of course not, but anything's better than watching you pout like a baby, you hypocritical son of—

She grabbed the cart angrily with an exaggerated nod, "Yeah, I'm sure."

They ran through the list as quickly as possible. The tone of his voice calling out items on their list made her wish she had come on her own.

He makes me wish I did a lot of things on my own.

She ignored the thoughts, grabbing the items herself to ensure they were correct, and bolted towards a register the moment they were done. Rather than conduct casual conversation as they waited in line, she began to scan the magazines.

Celebrity break ups – that sounds good. Somebody setting examples for people like me.

~*~

His eyes sailed to the long line beside them and immediately took notice of a happier couple. A couple about their age, held hands and gazed admiringly into one another's eyes, patiently waiting their turn.

Enjoy it while you can, buddy.

Forcing his eyes away from them, he set his eyes on Erica and tried to remember the last time she stared at him like that. They had met as freshman in college, and they had thought they were so ready for a relationship, perfection. But, heading into this five-year anniversary, everything had changed between them.

She probably doesn't even remember that it's coming up.

Her long black hair was casually thrown up, drastically different from the time she use to take fixing it, and her body dressed in sweats, the ultimate contrast to the fashion statements of before. He shook it off, handing his credit card to the cashier as his girlfriend loaded the cart and avoided his eyes.

"Have a good day, sir, and thank you for shopping with us."

Someone who knows how to say thanks, imagine that!

Offering a polite smile, he followed her to the car with an awkward silence residing between them.

~*~

"I got it."

She threw her hands up in surrender, stepping away from the trunk and to the passenger side of the car.

You don't want any help, fine with me.

Looking around the parking lot, she tapped her foot impatiently against the pavement and tightened her jaw.

He probably won't even open the door for me until his ass is in anyway.

She heard the trunk close and watched in disbelief as he walked halfway across the parking lot just to return the cart to its designated spot.

He can be polite to a female cashier, everyone in his new little church group, and even a freaking cart, but God forbid he shows me a hint of courtesy!

Once he had returned to the car, he checked the trunk again them proceeded to the driver's side of the car.

Un-believable.

Shutting her eyes tightly, she inhaled a deep breath of fresh air as he unlocked her door. She released it sharply, pulling the door open in frustration, and plopped down in her seat, slamming the door shut.

"Easy!"

She narrowed her eyes at him, remaining painfully silent.

"The last thing we need is to pay for fixing the car door."

Are you kidding me?

~*~

He saw her attention towards the world outside her window and hoped she would remain silent for the ride home. As usual, she disappointed him.

"Don't take the short cut."

Gripping the steering wheel angrily, he kept his eyes focused ahead, "It's quicker."

"It's not quicker. If you just take the normal route, like everyone else, you'd know that."

"Erica, would you just let me drive?"

"We have frozen stuff in the back!"

"All the more reason to take the short cut."

"I'm telling you, you're going the wrong way."

"Let me worry about the driving, all right?"

"Fine."

He was forced to stop abruptly, their argument nearly causing him to run the red light.

"So much for worrying about the driving, huh?"

Lord Jesus.

His faith had kept him from saying all the vulgarities he heard other men attribute to their women. But, for the moment, he almost asked God for a pardon. Thankfully, the light changed, and he proceeded.

What happened to my Erica?

The thought came to him unexpectedly.

You use to agree with me. You didn't argue with every single thing I had to say or do!

Another red light, he paused and glanced over at her.

"Dad says that equality between a man and woman is simple. You want to be treated like a queen, you have to treat your man like a king."

He grinned crooked towards her words, continuing through the back streets, but it vanished within an instant, when confronted by the road construction before them.

"So much for the short cut, huh, John?"

So much for being equal too.

~*~

They had put everything away in silence.

I shouldn't have said that. But I'll be damned if I apologize to you, John.

She watched in remorse as he squished the brown bags together and placed them in his freshly labeled recycle bin.

How the hell did we let it happen to us? We were supposed to beat everything.

Leaning slightly against the kitchen counter, she attempted to remedy the situation, "You want anything special for dinner?"

"Anything's fine with me."

"You sure?"

"Erica, whatever you feel like making is fine."

She bowed her head, somewhat wounded, and sighed heavily, "I'll just fry some meat and boil some bananas."

"Ah, you're favorite."

You use to think it was unique.

Meeting his eyes, she hugged herself with a tight grasp and shrugged, "Unless you tell me you want something else?"

"…no."

She could have sworn his tone softened with the answer, but she refused to believe it. It was even harder to trust as he casually kissed her cheek and exited the tiny kitchen, retreating to the one bedroom of their apartment.

Probably going to call one of his 'brothers' or 'sisters' to report the latest.

Retrieving a package of meat from the fridge, ready to cook from the ride home, she dropped it on the counter and stopped.

What am I doing? I can leave. There's nothing stopping me, not **one** *thing.*

The tears flooded her eyes as turned to face the closed bedroom door. Listening closely, she waited to hear his soft laugh and 'Amen' before going into their small living room. Out of clear spite, she found the busiest of her salsa music and turned it up to a nice *respectable* level. She moved in rhythm with the music, returning to the kitchen, and searched the cabinets for the perfect pot and pan. To her relief, he did not come out to react to her argument prompt. But, to her dismay, it meant he said nothing at all.

That's your problem! You're so saved that you have no heart! No fight, no spunk, just the perfect little puppet!

She continued with preparation of the meal, sure they would eat in silence.

You're not the man I fell in love with.

~*~

Standing to his feet, he began to gather the dirty dishes from the table, "Thank you."

See I know how to say it.

"You're welcome."

But you know how to say that, don't you?

He placed the plates next to the sink, filling one sink with hot soapy water, and glanced back at her, thinking of his phone call.

"Brother John, are you sure that you want to proceed with this relationship?"

"Well, I can't continue to live in sin. I have to marry her."

"Perhaps there's a reason things have changed. A reason you don't feel so connected anymore."

"I love Erica."

"I'm just suggesting you go to the Lord before truly committing to her, a woman who is so against your new life."

Snapping out of his thoughts, he looked to the dishes before she caught his stare.

"So, who were you talking to earlier? A boy or girl?"

Does it really matter?

Accepting her empty plate, he assured her calmly, "A brother."

"I suppose that should worry me too."

He gave her a brief look of dismissal before beginning to scrub.

"Are you ashamed of me?"

"What? Where did that come from?"

"You never invite them here, and you don't want me to meet them. What am I suppose to think?"

"I'm trying to show you respect. I know how you feel about religion."

"Right, so it's my choice."

Without another word she stepped out of the kitchen and into the living room.

~*~

It use to be their favorite past time, cuddling in the center of the couch and laughing at every available sitcom. But there was now a vacancy between them. One side of the couch belonged to her, complete with remote control and extra pillows. The other was his, complete with a reading light and the New Testament. A loud laugh escaped her in reaction to the verbal sparring on screen, but it died down when she saw he was in a world all his own.

Somewhere I can't go without giving myself up, like you did.

She rested her elbow on her arm of the couch and swallowed a lump in her throat, tempted to shut the television off and curl up next to him. Her eyes managed a sideward glance at him, taking in the vision that was her new and improved man.

Nothing had changed in his short brown hair, his hazel eyes, or his medium build. His voice was still that husky tone which melted her in every way. Yet there was something different in all the other things. The way he talked to her, the way he carried himself, and even in the way he touched her. The empty kisses he now left on her lips and skin stung. They were haunting memories of the past. Moments where he made her feel like the only woman, the only person, who mattered. Moments where he held her face in his hands, gazed deeply into her eyes, and when she thought she could take no more he would tenderly kiss her lips.

I'll let you back in my world, if you just let me be yours like the one more time.

The show ended, and she was done. Shutting off the TV, she stood to her feet. She stretched allowing him the opportunity to say good night or simply ask where she going. When he said nothing, she went to the bedroom without any explanation.

You're such a jerk.

She shut the door softly, holding a hand to her mouth, and forced tears back, refusing to give him the satisfaction of knowing what he was doing. Once she had gained her composure, she flipped on her nightstand light and ventured over to their tall dresser.

I'm going to remember you somehow, John. 'Cause, if I don't, I'll be gone before morning.

With this thought, she reached to the bottom of his T-shirts, knowing he kept the larger ones there, and pulled it out with a strong tug, hearing something fall to the ground. Her eyes shot to the floor, immediately spotting the little navy blue box, and time stood still. All she could remember was her mother's warning.

"Mija, if you remember anything I say –remember this, marriage is like buying a wig. You can't return it, it ends up ratted and looking all rotten, and you eventually need medication for what it does to your skin."

She picked the box up, too frightened to look inside, and shoved it back under the shirts of the bottom. Folding his shirt back up, thinking it might give her away, she placed it back under the opposite piled and hoped it looked normal. Sliding the drawer back in as quietly as possible, she grabbed one of her pajama short sets and changed at a rapid pace.

Why would he want to get married? We don't get along now!

She gathered her dirty clothes, tossing them to the hamper, then hesitantly went to bed.

There's no way we're getting married.

Throwing the covers back, she sat on the bed and felt tears begin to slide down her cheeks without any warning at all.

I love you, John, but not like this. Not like you are now.

She wiped her cheeks, spotting the picture nearby, and felt her heart sink.

That's gone. Those days are gone.

Laying the photo frame face down, she shut the light off. However, her mind wouldn't rest until she propped the frame back up and took another glimpse of their happier days. The second she did, she knew only one thing for sure.

But I'm not ready to let you go.

~*~

It had been at least an hour since she had went to bed, but he could not bring himself to join her right away. Carefully bookmarking his spot in his reading, he got up and shut everything down. He checked all the locks, all the burners, and windows before finally heading her way. Opening the door cautiously, he was happy to see her sound asleep in the moonlit glow of their bedroom.

This is the best part of the day, we've got nothing to argue about.

He took a deep breath, changing into some sweats, and tossed his clothes of the day into the laundry basket.

"Go to the Lord."

His friend's voice looped in his mind as he crawled in beside her, laying back and staring towards the ceiling. Their arguments, over everything, were his constant reminder that all had changed between them. The way they could sit for hours without a word, when they use to have trouble with any silence between them. Now, their bed was always cold. Their looks were always angry or sad. But neither of them had the courage to just walk out.

At least I don't.

He rolled his head towards her, needing to feel the way they use to. When she could give him a look, he had to smile. When her laugh was contagious and not irritating. When her touch made his skin burn with desire rather than remorse. He wanted her to see him the way she use to; wise and irreplaceable. Instead, she continued to focus on her college studies while he found himself inching towards training in the group and his new life.

How can I marry you? How can you be the woman I call my wife, when you're so against compromise?

In all honesty, he knew the marriage would probably never happen. But he had another week before the anniversary to decide. Frustrated by his own doubts, he faced his body towards her back and scooted close to her.

I love you, Erica. I know I do.

Wrapping his arm around her waist, he pulled her close to him and shut his eyes tightly. He caught the scent of her hair and skin, admitting to himself.

I can't let you go...not yet.

Perfection (2003)

I think it's funny that you don't understand,
Saying all the right lines doesn't make you a man,
I don't want someone who raps a perfect game,
I can only imagine how many girls heard the same.

You have it down when it comes to what meets the eye,
But I can just imagine what's going on inside,
I see the person you don't want me to see,
He's the one who impresses me.

That person was hurt and thinks they do it right by hurting someone else,
That person was broken and thinks getting it right means ignoring their self,
But when I see you again,
Please – let me see him,
Because that man could know the real me,
The one I don't want anyone to see.

Wanted (2003)

I want you to feel me while maintaining your distance,
I want you to hear me without forcing yourself to listen,
I want you to hold me and never use your arms,
I want you to protect me but let me see harm.

Trust me without judgment,
Love me not as a supplement,
Need me because of the heart that I carry,
Want me because I'm the type of girl you want to marry.

Look at me without blinders and love who you see,
I'm not the girls on screen and I like being me,
If you want something different than I suggest you walk on by,
Because I won't change to be the good girl living your lie.

My Forever Other

"Hard times make hard people, Yoyo."

His words rang through her ears like a school bell at the end
of class, bringing her to turn the knob of his apartment door and
send the door creaking open. Her feet crossed the threshold, the first
brave enough to do so since the accident, and immediately she felt
her heart had flopped to the hardwood floor. Her lungs begged for
a deep breath which she granted with tears as her eyes zigzagged
around at the surroundings. A home so normally filled with laughter,
with people, and the noise of a game or friendly fight was deadly
still. The counters were bare, without a trace of old food because
he hadn't cleaned the counters well enough. The floor was dusty
with the hair of a cat he swore he never wanted. Imprints usually
left by round backsides and dirty sneakers were gone completely
from the couch, no hint of presence since he left. Her shaky hand
weakly swung the door shut behind herself as she tried to grasp what
she was about to do, the only person strong enough to decide what
should stay and what should go.

No one else could do such a thing. No one else could believe
he was gone, never to run his mouth again. No one could accept he
wouldn't be there to set them straight about the harsh world. He left
them to do their own bidding. She suddenly felt as weak as them,
ill to her stomach and unwilling to accept the facts. She refused
to believe he would never walk through that door and shorten her
Yohance to Yoyo one more time. The tap of her heels against the
floor echoed through the dust as she made her way towards the
entertainment stand, his pride and joy.

There were very few things he had earned through his life
but what he had he displayed. A track trophy from high school, a
Chicago bear teddy bear he had won years ago, and a few pictures:
family, friends, and his girls, Yohance and Adela.

She felt the sob crawl out of her throat, unable to hear its cry,
when she found a picture of him with her sitting comfortable in one
of the stand's cubbies. Reaching to it, she found no energy to lift it
up and merely caressed his smile with a distant regret. Why had she
let him go? Why didn't she fight for him? She had no answers, even
now.

"Even if I don't say it, you have to know that I'm proud of you—you're the best person I know. The only one who has ever loved me unconditionally."

But she needed those words, not once but all the time. It was part of the reason she had walked away, unable to settle. At least that's what she had told herself. In this moment of solitude, robbed of his presence and surrounded by it all at once, she became guilt ridden. He had been there for her, the times she needed him most—unconditional. Yet she had rejected him for all the other times he had been absent, because of his confusion about them/because of his want for more than their high school romance, and she wanted to blame him even now. He was leaving her to clean his mess, to wrap up his life, and she was doing it without question. He was not her husband, her family, and he made one confused boyfriend for their brief courtship. Their friendship was an aged rollercoaster at best. It was scary almost life risking to board yet somehow they were the only two to consistent to line up, despite the risk of the shaky tracks.

Years had passed and their agreement to be the kind of friends who called every once in a while was always to painful for them both; because she had loved him with all the give she had as he loved her selfishly. She had wanted him while he wanted her to want more. When she had the opportunity to flee, she did and even then he supported her letting go.

"You'll always have it hard because pain is what creates greatness, and you can't stand being mediocre."

The creak of someone entering into the apartment made her head to whip around and face her familiar opponent. Standing in all of her perfection, her enemy gazed upon her with a mixture of emotions, the old friend and the new girlfriend battle was about to ensue. It stirred in her contact lenses. She shut the door with the soft tick of her tongue against the roof of her mouth then proceeded to attack.

"Yohance! I should have known you couldn't stay away." The sarcasm oozed out of her like a cloudy steam, rich with the distinct smell of bitterness and lies.

She stepped away from the picture, crossing her arms across her chest, and answered as calmly as her blood pressure would allow, "His mother asked me to come, Adela."

"Of course she did! After all, you are Yoyo." Adela dropped her purse and keys to the counter, standing proudly with her hands on her hips, "The plague on this family since he looked into those big puppy dog eyes, right?"

Laughing, she eased her shoulders back and pushed her chest out. She shot her eyes into Adela's, signaling with her stare to back off.

In response, Adela bowed her head with an awkward sigh, "Why couldn't you just stay away, huh? Even now, you have to remind everyone just how unhealthy he was."

She said nothing, but Adela snickered at this, quick to meet her eyes again with a warning equal in magnitude, "Don't you see what you had with him wasn't normal? It was pathetic and, even when my man dies, you're here! You just can't seem to stay out of—"

"I'm going to say this just once!" Her statement stopped her immediately, the tone which sent it ripping through the room caused Adela to free, "This is about him. Not about you or your insecurities, so just let it go."

"No, you don't get to be here!" Adela shouted, tears accompanying the passion of her words, as she pointed an accusing finger towards her, "I have his death, do you understand me?! You took way too much of him from me, and I will **not** let you take this! You either walk out that door on your own or I promise I will send you flying out the window!"

She felt her enemy's pain, the deep disturbance of being robbed of him, and her own tears begged to be released. However, her shame kept them at the gate. Her pride kept them locked in her chest. Rather than fight, she conceded once more. She pressed her lips together, causing them to leave a ghostly white on her lips, and made her exit as gracefully as possible while followed by Adela's strong sniffles and angry slam of the door.

Unable to deal with anymore of it, she ran towards the stairwell and raced down the four flights of stairs. Each step brought her closer to it. Each step reminded her he was gone; she no longer had a choice but to let go. She had to stop hoping. She had to stop feeling sorry for herself and what she had never had with him. Grabbing the rail, she would use a frustrated whirl to send her running down the next flight.

"I'll always be there."

A tear fell.

"You can always count on me."

Another fell.

"You are my family – you got me for life."

The rest followed out of her doe eyes as she collapsed on the last step, unable to breathe—unable to accept. She rested her head against the cool concrete and stared upward at the empty stairs, trying to grasp for something-anything- that would make this okay. Something like those caring eyes which understood every single wrong doing she had ever done. Something close to those warm hugs which surrounded her with nothing but love and acceptance.

Something likes his promises which felt like they were stronger than any rule she had ever lived by. Something just like him... something she was always looking for. When she came to the realization there was nothing, she dropped her head and the battle within had a clear victory. The guards had fallen, the gates had flooded, and her tears were screaming for his return.

"Yohance?"

The voice came out of nowhere, gaining Yohance's attention only when the stairwell door had shut behind her. Upon seeing the woman, she stood to her feet and reached out to find a strong embrace awaiting her.

"Aw, baby, I know." The words seemed to settled her only slightly, "I miss him too."

Yohance felt ashamed, immediately stepping back, and frantically responding, "I'm so—sorry I just—"

"It's all understood, honey. You don't have to explain."

"But—he was your son and—"

"Your everything." His mother stood there with glistening brown eyes, a familiarity of him within a gaze.

She dropped her head, wrapping her hands around her biceps, and admitted with a small shrug, "I don't have any right to be here."

"You have every right. I asked you to."

"That doesn't make it right."

"I'm his mama, ain't I?"

"Yes, but Adela's right. I should have stayed away."

"Adela's hurt."

She avoided his mother's eyes, staring away with the quiver of her lips.

"You gotta realize that it's never easy being second choice." Her words caused Yohance to stare at her in confusion, "He never gave her the chance be number one, and it's hard when you know that on your own but when everyone knows? Honey, everyone knowing that just makes things unbearable."

"But I didn't know." She trailed off, sensing his mother's disbelief, "I should go."

"He wouldn't want that."

Yohance looked upstairs, shrugging her shoulders, and smiled sadly, "He'd want a favor." His mother's sad bow of her head caused her to add, "He'd want to give Adela a chance."

When his mother began to nod, crying softly, she took her head in her hands and placed a soft kiss on her forehead, "Don't forget to call me, okay? You let me know if you need anything."

"Mm-hmm."

She stepped back once more, allowing his mother to memorize her confidence before she lost it beyond the door, and gave herself a chance to remember him. In his mother's eyes, she found him long enough to wave goodbye, and used the last bit of her loyalty to send her out of the apartment building.

Failed Wishes (2003)

Last night I uttered your name while wishing upon a star,
I wanted to hold it in my palm, thinking of you rather than leaving
it so far,
But the distance is what keeps me from falling for you completely,
And for that I thanked it.

I said your name while tossing a coin into a cool fountain of hope,
But its cold nature kept you from warming my soul and helped me
cope,
I'm not waiting for your call,
Prevented from that life altering fall,
And for that I thanked it.

As I was returning the charm on my necklace to its proper place,
I whispered your name repeatedly while picturing your face,
And its order caused me to leave things as they were,
It helped me realize what we want isn't what always needs occur,
And for that I thanked it.

While blowing away the feather of a cloudy flower
I made a request to have you,
But as it flew away it hit me that things don't always fly
As we want them to,
It led me to turn my back on us
And find my path solo,
With no compromises to make
And no second heart telling me no,
And for that I thanked it.

On my knees
I sat and prayed for some kind of sign,
Not knowing that my solution
I would have to find,
And all these failed wishes were telling me something us,
Yet I'm still making plenty of wishes
Despite what it may cost.

Our Future (2003)

A year from now I saw you and had to rejoice,
A year since I'd seen my friend and heard his lovely voice,
I wanted to memorize your face once again,
As we exchanged numbers and promised to call with each day's
end.

Five years from now we bumped into each other
and I ran into your awaiting arms,
Five years since I had felt that security
protected from any harm,
I wanted remember the warmth which consumed all I was,
Knowing we'd be separated for some reason
Beyond our cause.

Ten years from now I met you
upon your out of the blue request,
And I showed off my ring to you
Showing you I had finally found my best,
And you said you were happy for me
maintaining that gorgeous grin,
Only after I promised you – no matter what
I'd always be your friend.

Eleven years from now I saw you
Through misty eyes,
Making my way down the aisle –
a toughie in girly disguise,
And you were happy for me
because I asked you to be,
Only as I pledged my love to another man,
You realized our friendship would have to end.

Fifteen year from now I saw you
as we watched and adored my kids,
You told me you were proud and happy for me
even if I was his,
And as we sat to speak of how good life could be,
Both of us knew the happiness belonged to me.

Ninety years from now
I saw you after our wheel chairs crashed,
And we talked about how different our paths were
to so often clash,
And you told me it wasn't coincidence,
Your love for me had never faded
Not even for a minute.

And I wondered how for ninety years we couldn't see,
Wondered how different our lives could be.

Real World Worries

No Way Out, Just One Way In (1995)

Take each day you have like it's all your time,
Don't fill it up with guns, drugs, and crime,
Cause I did too and look where I am today,
I'm learning all my lessons the hard way,
Because now I am on my way out, but just before I leave,
Let me share with you what I've received.

My friends dying in front of me,
Nothing I could do but wait and see,
Nothing I could do for help but scream and yell,
And right there I should have learned before I got to this hell.

But no I concentrated all my concern,
I just could not learn,
I was looking to get the guys who shot my friend,
Soon – had to be their end.

We went to the funeral that day,
Of course I had nothing to say,
As I saw the coffin go down…down…down,
I thought not me - I won't go down in the ground,
Then I thought why him – why now,
Instead of crying, I just lowered my brow,
I saw his mom with endless tears,
Recognizing her biggest of fears,
I saw his father wipe her face – wanting nothing more than to help
her cope,
Knowing he had wanted his son to succeed – he held even higher
hope,
He had wanted his boy out of the gangs and off dope,
But his son couldn't walk away – hung himself with that rope,
Though dad only wanted the best for him,
He could never understand no way out – one way in.

I left then,
To avenge my friend,
A girl, poor girl, was caught in the crossfire,
I got out of the car and knelt beside her,
"Why" she asked "I didn't do a thing,"
I had nothing except "Wrong place, wrong time."
Her brother got me back – one bullet in the chest,
It's only now I realize I'll finally rest.

Yesterday (2003)

I just got the news about your death yesterday,
I was completely blown away,
Right out of the present and far into the past,
I saw your smile consuming your face,
And the warmth of your heart filling the surround space,
I remember your bright hair and light humor setting off our friendship,
How I cringed at your piercings and that evil grin on your lips,
But what I remember the most is that one night,
Suddenly maintaining that smile was a fight,
I quickly found out you weren't happy all the time,
Sometimes felt like no one cared and you were losing your mind.

And though I gave you my number to call if you ever needed anything,
You never did,
And though I consistently asked if you need to talk,
You never did,
And I considered myself a friend?
What a fool I am.

Because I found out about your death yesterday,
I began mourning you yesterday,
It's been sometime since your death,
And I just found out yesterday.

So I ask myself if I was truly your friend,
How could I not know of your death,
I thought you had transferred to another school,
Thought I would soon see you on the big screen,
But all that's left now is the memory
of that damn fairy costume you wore and your big city dreams.

Mommy Dearest (2009)

Memories of a mother who held me as a child
are what I cling to even as you miss the most important days of my
life
I recall the one time we baked a cake together each time you miss
my birthday
I thought back to the single conversation we had about boys the day
I married the man of my dreams
I laughed at a distant image of you chasing me as I ran down an
immaculate hall the moment my baby boy took his first walk
I cried, surrounded myself with a long ago embrace we shared, when
I lost my closet friend

Through everything, I have struggled to see your side
Longing to be the daughter you always wanted
in hopes you would accommodate my wants and turn into a different
mother
One who didn't criticize my simple choice in clothing or life choice
in my marriage
One who didn't call me a crybaby when I questioned the past
One who never held my rebellion against me, instead applauded my
courage in standing alone
One who understood that no matter how old I got, I was still the
child and she was still the adult

Instead, you continue to miss the important days
You neglect my needs for a relationship with you
And you blame your loneliness on my ability not to apologize
I wish you the best in your life because you are my blood
I pray you'll change your ways and create a circle of family around
you
But while you're working to have it all, recognize that I already
possess the life of a queen
And I did it all without you

Fucked Up Fairytale (2002)
Dedicated to all of the 'Fallen'

After all was said and done,
The whole crowd focused on one,
All were curious to see what would emerge,
What belonged to the people and what was hers.

Shattered, broken,
The woman gathered herself to a stand,
Staring in disbelief,
The crowd failed to extend a hand.

Her long, unruly curls insisted the blinking of her eyes,
The crowd was shocked, astounded she hadn't died,
Even with only a sheet around her,
She stood proud in bare feet,
Jutting her chin to the air,
Impressing all despite the dirt smearing her cheek.

But his claims that she wanted it too caused the crowd to assume it
was true,
Doubt their town's hero was something they just couldn't do,
Pushing through the crowd she listened to the people cry 'slut' and
'whore,'
These ignorant fools feeding into the belief she was nothing more.

They make this harder for her than that one night,
Every day the small town continues their abuse,
Clipping her wings to make themselves right,
Believing she's here only for his use.

Fallen from the sky,
An angel not meant for you,
Everybody's favorite guy,
May he pay when his life is through,
You took her life for just one night,
One question…was it really worth it?

Wave

"Daddy, I need your help."

Her words came out shaky, dripping with fear and desperation. And it was impossible to ignore his suspicions any longer. He had done it for so long, even as their afternoon talks were widdled to a once a week tea sit down. He said nothing. Somewhere, he had just imagined it was in his head. He had held out hope for her, hoping her life had resulted better than his, hoping his daughter would be smarter heading into marriage.

Instead, he stared at a frail young woman who once was a vibrant old soul. Her luscious strawberry blond curls had become stringy, straight, and strange. Her full glowing cheeks were sunken in and blemished. Her blue eyes once big and bright were now shifty and dark searching impossibly among the floor. Her posture had lost its height, leaving her old comfy sundress to look more like a tent on her ever shrinking frame. Where was his little girl? The one who chased the seagulls along the seashore; her long curls frantically following her with a bounce, her laughter dancing around him. Even now, each time he closed his eyes, he could still feel the sun against his skin while he watched his angel bask in all of life's simplicities.

"Daddy, please, we don't have a lot of time."

Staring into her frightened gaze once more, he offered a gentle yet unsure smile, "Anything for my shortcake."

She released a relieved breath and threw her arms around him, whispering, "We have to be quick and quiet."

Her warm embrace left him cold as she cautiously made her way out of the room, signaling she would only be a moment. His smile had faded the moment she was out of sight, and his eyes wandered the room around him. Eventually, they set upon the picture hovering over the fireplace, one of his daughter and her husband. His eyes became fixated on the older man's hands snapped onto his daughter's shoulders. He could remember shaking those hands on many occasions, including the day he consented to their marriage. There was no way to forget a touch so cold, the roughness it left even as it disappeared. Then there were those eyes, ebony of the purest kind, so dark that you could barely make out a pupil. To this day, he found it hard to look into them even a picture. Avoiding the man's gaze altogether, he found his eyes resting on the beaked nose which shadowed thin lips. There it was. The crow had latched onto his daughter, making promises which he could never keep and giving her no escape.

"Let's go."

The warmth of her hand on his had sent his feet following her out of the room, yet his eyes could not leave the picture until it was completely out of sight. Within the blink of an eye, they were in the ol' red pickup and he finally noticed the bag on her lap.

"We have to get going before he gets off that phone. Gas it!"

Struggling for a moment to start, the truck eventually did its job; they were racing toward the open gate doors. He stared at the road just beyond the gate, not nearly as hopeful as his girl and tried to ignore the feeling emerging from his stomach. It was overwhelming him just as the sea water use to be to his bare feet. How would he care for her? How would she live if something happened to him? And why, why did she have to be like her… like that woman.

Glancing over at his child, he could almost see his runaway bride; the one who had walked out on them when Shortcake was only a baby; the one who had left a clueless man to raise a little woman. He almost wondered if it was his fault she had never really grown up, never married a man until the man had directly dealt with her father. With all of these thoughts, his foot had shifted from the gas to the brake.

"Daddy, what are you doing?"

"I--I can't do it."

"What? Yes, yes, you can. Let's just go home."

"He's your husband."

"He's the enemy. He--" She stopped short, her eyes darting to the gates they had nearly escaped, and her voice became rushed, "Oh no, daddy, he's closing them. You—you gotta go! Floor it!"

"I can't—I can't take care of both of us, Shortcake. He'll—he'll give you a good life."

"Don't you get it? There is **no** life here!" Her eyes became glossy with betrayed tears, "…I wanna go home, Daddy… to the little shack and the ocean."

"You deserve better than that."

"…I don't deserve this."

Before he could respond, the passenger door had opened beside her. There her husband stood, letting out a slim slick smile under the hook of his nose and offering a small nod to his father-in-law. His daughter's lower lip began to quiver, just as it had when he use to deny her the prettiest doll in the store, and he felt two feet tall.

Swallowing a thick lump of indignity, he hung his head low with a whisper, "I'm so sorry, Shortcake."

"If you leave now, if you leave without me…"

"…I won't be back."

With that, her husband's cool voice had hit the air, "Come, dear, we have a dinner engagement to get ready for."

With the last ounce of courage he had, her father took one last look into her betrayed eyes and assured her, "Everything I've ever done was for you."

She said nothing while taking her husband's hand, bringing her bag over her shoulder, and getting out of the truck. The slam of the door said it all.

~*~

It had been months since he had seen his daughter. There had been no call. No letter. No hint that she could forgive him. He was left to his lonely life by the sea. Her gaze still haunted him, that one last look of disappointment ate at his very core. But he held on strong, searching for some connection to her memory. However, he had paid the ultimate price because every time he looked back, he could no longer see the little girl; he only saw the hateful beauty she had grown up to be. Her laugh was gone, her curls no longer danced in the wind, and her light had completely vanished. So even when the waves tickled his toes, the sun caressed his cheeks, the sea had lost all of its magic.

The Perv & His Serve (2006)

My feelings for you are like a light switch on and off,
It could be as cold as the hand that makes you turn and cough,
You did it to yourself by walking around that swell,
And I know my girl played a part – she will be sentenced to the same
hell,
I will cut you both loose,
But smoothly as not to give you an ego boost,
And she will drive you mad as I smile in the background,
You will dance with her til the music dies down –
just another clown.

You'll be just another name on a very long list,
And please spare me when you're boiling pissed,
Or if by chance you play her,
Move in quickly just to lay her,
Don't be surprised if I act the same,
Because you have quickly revealed your game.

You beautiful speech has become transparent,
Your booty call is the only signal you've sent,
But you'll both get yours eventually,
Or end up a perfect fucking family.

My First Love (2008)

Anger, frustration and disappointment at how you see me,
Funny how a conversation can make me see you have no clue
It's like no matter many times I say it
you don't think I'll set you free,
It's a test you give me consistently,
Like clockwork set to push me to cross the line.

Like you think from you I'll never run,
Unaware of tracks I've already spun,
It's as though you think I'm naïve,
I don't see the man or obstacles in front of me.

You have shown me that your 'love' and understanding of me has
its limits,
So I'm to break it down real clear by the time this is finished!

When it comes to you
I do see crystal clear,
A man of huge talents and pride
ruled by little boy fear,
A man who has allowed the people who hurt him
the most control of who he is and his beautiful heart,
A man who consistently hurts the woman who has stood strong
despite his attempts to rip their relationship apart,
A woman who could easily be the very bitch he wanted
but didn't because his pain caused her to be haunted.

Even as she stood a fool – broken hearted- then
Sent away for the woman in the bedroom (Merry Christmas),
She put her bullshit pride to the side
Because she wouldn't be his doom,
She tried not to be like every woman
who played and hurt him in the past,
She was determined to let them go as a couple
and make a friendship last.

Yeah, she was hurt when the girls jumped him at the club,
Who wouldn't be a little stung
at the loss of a first love,
But she kept going
determined to show him love was deeper
than what was received and was all in what was given.

Now as I sit here
Writing these words
I realized where I messed up,
Put expectations and hopes in you only to be truly fucked.

You still don't realized that I loved you unselfishly,
That I always made love to you
and gave you a piece of me,
I trusted you to love and appreciate all of me,
You were supposed to see the good and bad
allow me back my purity,
Where I could love a man
No matter who he was to me
Because he would never pass judgment upon me,
You've become like every other friend in my life
who comes around only when they need me,
Whether it's money, to feed your ego, or simple obligation,
You've become just like them part of my frustration.

Is it because you think I'm weak
that our relationship turned into this,
Where you think all is better
with a little forgive me kiss,
I told you if you think you can find better than me
go on – I dare you,
At the end of the day
it'll turn out my way and I won't be waiting for you.

The one person who understood my job was to make it easier
and show you real love,
It wasn't about being your girl
instead I was the one who would have stayed true to her word
and backed you up,
And after all this time
In your eyes
I can never do right by what I do or say,
I suggest you look in the mirror for you
See what I can do
And see that you pushed me away.

I wanted to tell you so much
but you were always running to pack,
I never really told you who I am or what I been through because of
the track.

I didn't tell you about the girl "touched"
not once but twice,
I didn't tell you how hard it was for
when the girls called her easy instead of nice,
I didn't tell you about the girl
who had to realize her beauty,
After boys talked about nothing
but her boobs and booty.

I didn't tell you about the boys
who tried to use daddy as a way to get into her skirt,
Or how, for a long time, she felt like
Mommy's mistake and how like hell that hurt,
Or how it wasn't only in the hospital
that she saw her daddy die,
It was years of cleaning him
and having an angel as her number one guy.

Or how she heard and saw her cousin get beat,
Only to have her run back to him just down the street,
Or how stupid this girl felt for loving a man
she probably knew nothing about,
Or about how she knew "Gilly"
Slept with a lot of girls in route,
Or how she felt whenever he blew her off,
Consistently wondering why for him
she had gone so soft.

At the end of the day, of this,
You can't see who I am,
And I'm thankful you just let me go,
And you finally realized that
true love you'll never know.
The only reason I stuck in so long
was because my love for you ran so deep,
But you decided and what we are
to both of us is nothing to keep.

At the end of the day
the biggest gift you could give me - you did,
You walked away before I was trapped
in a worthless relationship or stuck with your kid.
Love to you always,
Thank you for allowing us our separate ways.

Faith in the Faithless (2009)

My heart is still cracked from the repairs I had to make to it
after I sent you away
Unable to take your hateful words,
your talent for making me feel so small
Refusing to give you a third chance to put a hand on me,
your last effort at taking the last of who I was

Never did I imagine those big brown eyes
would manipulate me with crocodile tears
Never did I think those muscles
would be used to show me I was weak in every way
Never did I question the relationships lost in the past
could trust everything my dark angel told me
as he swore every one of them had used all he had

No one ever wanted you for you
No one ever showed they could be trusted
No one ever stuck around and proved they were there only for you
No one ever did anything without a secret motivation
and that's why you couldn't trust me

But I trusted you
Even as you turned my every doubt or question into a fight
Even as you took my money and my pride
Even as you placed your hands around my neck,
robbing me of my last ounce of innocence

I gave you every piece of me, physically and emotionally
Only to be depleted to nothing
You got to walk away with well wishes from me
as I was too afraid to be the bad person
I left a message on the cell phone
as I was afraid to look you in the eye
I'm glad you left me alone
as I requested, a gift from God in your disappearance

You were toxic to me
yet somehow taught me a lesson
I will never be with anyone
until I can stop blaming men for all that you did

And the Beat Drops...

Booties bouncing to the beat; hips grinding in time with their feet; and eyes wandering the place like there's no time to spare. I swear this isn't a meat market. It's an auction. Women bidding with their strongest scent, shortest skirts, and lowest cut shirts. And all my boys hoping that their shower lures that little mama as much as the drinks they're buying. Not me though, I'd rather stay here. Just lean against the bar, bob my head to the music, and wait for one of those minis to sashay my way. Then there are guys like my homie, D. He just walks right up to them, no hesitation, and pulls up to their back like one grind is gonna get them to turn around. I keep trying to tell him that women are more like dudes these days. They want what they want, they go for it, and they don't really want him. But more power to him. I got nothing but love for that little white boy, flyest one I've ever known. Besides, he can't be doing any worse than that dude across the room, whispering in that little Latina's ear while she winks at the baller passin' by. And you know what, I don't have to know her to *know* her. I've meet *her* every time I come to the club. The second that dude stops mackin', she's going to follow that 50 look alike right to the middle of the dance floor. She'll be working that dance for all its worth, smiling that flirty little grin then getting into his ride...as long as it's expensive. If it's not, she won't be able to "leave" her girls inside. He might get the digits though, just because she'll think he's going to get the money one day. Holla!

Gotta shake my head man, if everyone in here knew what I did? Shoot...it would be a whole different game. These cats just don't understand, but I get it. I got on that train a long time ago and rode it out of the station. You know, one time, I had a dream about getting married. Church and everything, Mama would have been proud. I'm watching the finest Halle Berry lady make her way to me, and I'm thinking this is it. Next thing I know, she's grabbing my boy D's hand! Just a dream, but the point still applies. Some dreams need to stay dreams, and some dreams just can't help but turn into nightmares. Speaking of which, looks like that little JLo is heading after 50. Ah...it use to feel good when I was right, and now it's just too damn predictable.

And where's D? Buying yet another shortie a drink. Damn... he just don't learn. Did you know that girls are even paying these days? I got no problem with that. But women even do that harder than men. Trust me, a man's expectations are far less when expenses include a combo number four. It must be getting late, I've heard this song before and some of these ladies are looking a little tipsy. But we can't leave this spot until D's had enough, so I better chill out. Besides, I'm getting the feeling I'm not alone right now.

Up there, VIP section, not too bad. I gotta thing for big Bambi eyes anyway. Let's give her a little look, and there ya go. Not a bad smile. Hmm…those exclusive girls are a little more reserved, I might have to approach. Nah, I'll see her next week I'm sure. A little wait always makes things sweeter.

Book Learning (2009)

Salute my accomplishments and forget my shortcomings
Applaud my ability to stand up after being pushed to the ground
Validate my strengths and help me overcome my obstacles
Encourage my learning especially in my mistakes

Motivate me as your student and I will teach things outside of the textbook
Eliminate what you think you know about me and become my teacher in life

A True Hispanic Experience

Anita furiously let her pen flow, reliving the events of yet another horrid high school day, and tried to make sense of a subject which infuriated her so.

How can I embrace a culture which has refused me? Sure, my last name says Cortez but if I can't pass my own Spanish class, how can I claim to be Latina? And how could my family not teach me the language of our people while I was growing up, yet jump on every bandwagon there is? Do you know how embarrassing it is to be known as 'white girl' Anita? They don't even call me gringa because they're so sure I won't get it!

Slamming her diary shut, she threw the book and her pen across the room. The tears were burning her throat, but she refused to let them make their way to her eyes. She took a minute, looking at her walls dressed with posters among off white paint. Each one reminding her how Americanized she was, every boy she fantasized about was yet another blue-eyed all American boys. At moments like this, she never hated her own wants more. Her eyes then travelled back to her Spanish notebook, full of words she could never announce properly and structures she would never understand. Anita recalled the only kind words she had that day, spoken by an opinion she respected… her Spanish teacher.

"Maybe you can go to your mother for help? If she speaks it, I'm sure she'd love to share it with you."

Reluctantly, Anita grabbed the book and made the long journey downstairs. She paced herself to the kitchen where her mother was preparing dinner, forcing herself not to turn around. When she had reached the kitchen, she spotted her mother chopping away. Anita paused, staring at a woman she respected more than any other. Her mother had worked hard for the family, hard to keep them together and striving. But in this situation, she was sure her mother would want no part. Anita had been to her a few times, trying to practice her Spanish in vain. Her mother had to hang her head, seeming ashamed at each word her daughter butchered simply by uttering it in 'her American accent'. Mama had defended her, mentioning something about since she had not been taught – how could she know. Meaning, if family had not said it, it could never be right or perfect.

Anita wanted to make her proud, let her see that somehow her daughter could accomplish both being Latina and American.

This gave her Spanish class a whole new meaning. Looking to her notebook once more, she persuaded herself to study one more night in solitude and beat the entire language. Yet just as she was about to turn around, her eyes connected with her mother's.

Offering a warm smile of reassurance, her mother greeted quietly, "Hola."

But Anita could think of one response before running back to her room, "Adios."

Scatterbrain (2003)

I'm getting tired,
I'm getting sick,
Wondering what happened to my skin,
Which was once so thick.
I can't take it anymore,
Everyone's got a problem,
Coming to me for answers,
Like I got 'em.

No matter what I do,
It isn't the right way,
I'm getting in over my head,
No matter what I say.

My stress and frustration are at an all time high,
No one gives me an ounce of credit while I'm walking by,
Every time I say not again,
Another fake ass person lets themselves in,
Every time I drop things at night I've got to pick up the next day,
Being a good person so far has done nothing and my luck doesn't
sway.

I want to put my fist through a wall,
But I can't afford to get it fixed,
I want to be a part of the world,
But I can't get in the mix.

I want to fight you half the time,
But I can't go to jail or pay the court fine,
I'm getting tired and sick,
Don't know what medicine to seek,
I'm going to lose it with one more diss,
Driven to the ground and oh so weak.

How many things do I have to do before I get some respect,
I dish it out but myself often neglect,
I want to run and never come back,
I want you to forgive me and cut me some slack.

Yeah, you've got issues,
But you don't have mine,
Yeah, your life's bad,
But I'm walking this fine line.

You wonder why I say things to tick you off,
Wonder why I have nothing nice to say to you,
Then think about the thoughts I don't bother to speak,
Maybe afterward you'll know what to do.

You're right I'm confusing,
I planned it all along,
Figure me out,
And get another reason to move on.

Little by little its building and pushing me over the edge,
Had no idea after losing him I was standing on this ledge,
I keep dusting myself off while getting off the ground,
Where are those friends who claimed to be down?

There's only so much this human being can take,
Sick of people claiming to have part in the self I make,
Sick of people asking questions when something already went down,
Claiming they wanted to help when the answer I've already found.

Sick of people offering their two cents and giving me advice,
When I already took a chance and rolled the dice,
How to trust after that one tragic loss,
Which taught me never to rely on someone else?

Where were my friends when things started to crumble,
What about my M.I.A. family while his health began to tumble,
Where was anyone while I cried at his side,
Where was God as he slowly died?

I'm losing faith in everything I use to know,
Feeling those doubts start to grow,
Hey Scatterbrain,
Just maintain.

Issues for Brando (2009)

You'd be surprised
how many people
quote "Grease"
as a classic
yet have never seen
you in anything
except the Godfather.

You'd also cringe
at people
who think Casablanca
is the only black & white
that ever mattered.

To have never seen
a waterfront
or street car,
You'd be surprised.

And while the stars
are doing anything
for attention,
the movies suffer.

As the writers work
at creating scripts
for a name,
there are no more Yous,
De Niros, or Paccinos.

And as it becomes
all about the money
less about the art,
there are no more
contenders.

Another Day, Another Dollar

People think it's so easy. Ha! What do you know? What would you really know about dressing up every day, when it's hot enough to fry an egg on the sidewalk? What would you know about being kicked in the ass by some little six-year-old who may be your boss one day? Ah…you wouldn't know. You *don't* know. You know I used to have dreams too. I used to think the world was my oyster.

Oyster…ha! That's something *they* feed you to try and inspire you, knowing damn well it ain't true. But I know. I know the world is waiting to swallow us alive, but that's why they stuck me in the suit. Because who's ever gonna listen to the jerk in the costume?

It was noon, and I needed a drink. So far, my day had gone just *lovely*. I had two babies with their stinky, fly enticing diapers to hold as they cried and screamed at the top of their lungs. I had an old couple, hard of hearing, ask me for over an hour about the directions to another country. And already two rug rats had kicked me in the ass.

This is my life. Ay yi yi, how pathetic. I didn't want this. I didn't want these white-gloved hands or these damn mouse ears. I wanted to be…an *actor*. I wanted to do a movie so good it made De Niro wet his pants. I wanted to win an Academy Award just so I could tell them to shove it. I wanted to travel the world, marry a model, and (before this job) have ungrateful kids of my own. That's over. Now, I just want to clock out and grab a drink with The Dog.

The sun was blazing, but I knew better than to pass out. These kids are vultures! They see a dead body, and they'll devour it! I don't get it. What sick, maniacal, demented mind thought of a whole "world" dedicated to these little bastards? If it were up to me…let's just say it's a good thing it's not. And parents, why do parents bring their already spoiled off-spring to revel in torturing me? As if life wasn't already doing a great job. They're Satan's spawn sent to punish me for some evil deed for which I can never redeem myself. I swear if one more kid—

"Hey, mouse!" I turned to see a brat standing there, his thumbs pressed to his temples as his hands waved and his tongue stuck out at me.

"You listen to me you little--" I began as I leaned towards him, suddenly feeling that familiar unbearable pang in my swollen behind.

I spun around to the other little flying monkey who is disguised as a little girl with blond, curly pigtails.

"I know where you live, and I'm gonna--" For a change of pace, I felt a crushing pain on my foot, "Ow!!!" I groaned as the little demons hopped away, proud of what they had done to me.

Yes, this is what I have to look forward to every day.

I took my seat on the nearest bench, hoping that pimple-faced boss of mind doesn't give me any crap. And the world passed me by as I tried to come to terms with the facts.

I would never escape this hell. I would never travel the world, and I would have to deal with the substitute a few blocks away. I would never marry a model unless she appeared in Hustler. I could never shove that Academy Award or make De Niro wet his pants. No, I could only count down the three hours left until poor Ernie came to take over the shackles.

~*~

His day looked like it had gone as good as mine.

"I swear I'd like to use those little cretins as footballs. Who's with me?!" The Dog slumped in his seat on the bench.

She batted her eyelashes, messing with an earring, "I think they're sweet."

"Shut up, Princess, no one asked you," I told her as I sat beside him.

The Dog bent down and retrieved his comforter from his bag. He held the fat cigar to his nose and deeply inhaled its stinky scent, drool cornering at the side of his mouth.

She responded with a light, calm tone, "Now, if I punched you in the mouth, would I be wrong?"

I love Mona. She knows how to make a man cower. And you gotta respect that in a woman.

I smiled sarcastically, "What would you know? The little girls admire you, and little boys wanna marry you when they grow up. You and all the other skirts have it easy. The rest of us around here have a *whole* other level of crap to deal with. Don't compare the two, sweetheart."

"Well, Terrance, if you stopped threatening the kids maybe, just maybe, they would be nice to you," she said.

I shrugged, "I've cut down."

"Yeah, since boss warned you again," The Dog laughed, clearly not helping my case.

"Nevermind that. When we going out, Mona?" I asked her as she slipped on a heel.

"Not any time soon, let's just leave it at that."

She flirted with me. I knew she did. That sneaky smile signaled to me, she was mine. A few more hundred times of asking, and she would be all over me.

She smoothed her dress and sighed, "Have a good night, fellas, try not to drink the bar out of business."

"You want me, you know you do!" I called after her as she sashayed away, "Ah..."

I'll bet if I could keep a drink from passing these perky lips, Mona would give me a chance. But could she ever warm me as much as Jack Daniels? I don't think so.

I punched out after The Dog, and we were on our way out. But before the two of us could escape, his high pitched voice stopped us.

"Wait a minute, guys."

We turned to be greeted by the weasel highness. His greasy hair, butter yellow teeth, and pimpled skin bloomed under the florescent light.

"I noted a few unscheduled breaks you took today. I'm gonna have to dock you."

"I'll dock you."

The Dog held me back, and that pat to my shoulder assured me the kid wasn't worth it.

We merely swallowed our pride and shuffled out.

~*~

As I look around the bar, I feel pathetic. I realize all my friends are as hopeless as I am. It's sad, it's weird, and it's never where I thought I would be.

Nothing comes easy to me, never has, but I was hoping there would come a time, a day, hell a minute. Just once, when Terrance Ryan got a break, you know?

It's too late now.

We sit here, and we talk about something more depressing than our glory days or our fallen dreams...we speak of now. We've all adjusted to this life, and we've somewhat come to terms with it.

With a glance to my right, I see my two partners in pathetic. For a second, it's impossible to see them, all you see is the suits. Imagine that, The Duck and The Dog at the smoky bar with a shot in hand and their head hung low.

Shaking off the image quickly, I look towards that soothing elixir and smile to myself. As it makes its way down, I can literally feel a calmness wash over me.

The Dog licks his lips as though he had almost lost a drop then continues with his rant, "What I don't understand is why I, a dog, don't get a little more respect than that damned bear. He's named after crap for Christ sake. And me! I'm loyal and faithful. He just sits around complaining and stealing honey."

"And you say you're not an actor," I mumble, signaling the bartender for another.

"To hell with acting."

"Why? It's part of the job," Don chimes in.

The duck...no one knows his real name, the poor bastard just kind of tags along.

Don hiccups after his sentence and leans against the counter, barely maintaining his seat on the stool.

The three of us sit at the counter as only a small addition to the bums which fill the bar, including Luna.

You can smell her coming from a mile away. I don't know how in the world she manages to get so many drinks from men, but I have a feeling it has something to do with making her go away.

She was once a model, or so she claims, and had a great life until her agent stole from her...

"Leaving me high and dry," The Dog, Don, and I shout in unison, helping her finish her rant as she slurs her words.

"What is with you, Luna? Why can't you just go home!" I snap, "We've got problems of our own. Buy your own damn drinks!"

Luna begins her pout, crocodile tears filling her misty blue eyes, "I thought you were my friends. Why you being so mean?"

"Fine! You wanna drink." I pull out a few bucks and toss it her way. "Just do it and leave us alone."

"Thanks, Terri." She stumbles and fumbles while I shrug her off.

"Just get, Luna."

She takes the money, shoving it down her shirt, before making her drunk strut away.

Don exhales, swirling his glass, "I'm trying to decide what's worse. Hearing that woman complain or being paid to get kicked in the ass."

"What planet considered that women a model?" The Dog frowned, staring at her in disgust and disbelief as she began to pester other patrons.

I can't help but laugh. "You actually think she was a model?"

"Well, you were an actor, weren't you?"

Again, I have to laugh. "Since when do you give a damn about Luna and when I take cracks at her."

"I'm just saying we all got something."

"Right," Patting his shoulder, I lean over slightly, "why don't you go help Luna find that money I gave her?"

He pushes me away angrily as Don and I share a laugh. And it seemed like hours before The Dog spoke again.

"Nobody's better than anybody here. These are our people, Ter." Motioning towards our surroundings, he says with a crooked grin, "This is it. Take it or leave it."

At that moment, it really hit me. Take it or leave it.

What a concept, huh? Just walk away. Why don't I just quit this job, quit this life, and move on...to something.

I literally feel the bravery swell in my chest, "I'm gonna quit. I'm leaving."

Don shakes his head and The Dog slams his palm against the counter repeatively, both bursting into laughter.

The Dog calms his laughter, pushing my shot glass away from me, "You're done."

"I'm serious."

"Yeah, yeah, you get *this* serious every time you've tipped a few back." The Dog glances over at Don, chuckling as he motions back at me, "I told you he can't hold his liquor worth a damn."

My jaw and weary muscles tighten in response to this.

How could they doubt me? How could they not see the severity of my decision? Why can't they just believe me?

I shouldn't have to be stuck with this. I'm not defeated. There's something out there for me. I know it.

I'm decided. "Anything's better than this."

"Man, we go through this **every time**. When are you just going to accept it? Like everyone else, you're stuck here. And, trust me, there's nobody checking out your mouse act."

Damn that dog, and he wonders why the kids like the fat ass bear better.

"It's not like anything's changed. You're not going anywhere, and neither are we. This is our life sentence, nobody's gonna serve it for us."

Don raises his glass to The Dog, trying to constrain another hiccup, "Ere--'ere."

"You're wrong." I retrieve my shot glass, shaking my head, and mumble angrily, "I'm done. I'm leaving."

They merely roll their eyes, returning to their drinks.

I have to quit this job before it kills me. And I'm going to do it first thing tomorrow. I'm saying goodbye to the suit.

Womanly Wiles

My Own Knight (2001)

Life can be just so deceiving,
You think you're alive – but you're just leaving,
The people around you don't know who you are,
You think you're so close – but you're only too far.

Life is strange and all too funny,
You feel the rain yet look back to see that it's sunny,
Do you ever wonder if someone understands,
Do you ever wish you could touch their hand,
Do you ever lie around in a daze,
Wondering why you're living this maze?

Well I often wonder this and so much more,
Wonder when my prince will come and allow me to adore,
But then I realize there may not be that horse and knight,
That there may come a point where I stand alone to fight,
This point where I hold the sword to protect myself,
I don't need a man – or a friend – I am my help,
I'll hold my head proud,
I will fight off in a voice all too loud,
In the distance I'll recall those who love and care for me,
But before my eyes my reflection is all that I'll see.

I gotta look at and support that girl in the mirror,
I have to overcome and calm her every fear,
I'm the one who has to keep sane,
I have to push back stupidity so she can keep her brain,
And if I have to lift my sword and fight every single day,
Even if I have to ward all insecurities away,
Then that's what I'll do – my sword will never lay,
I would do anything for that girl looking back at me to stay.

The Terrible D's

She held the bra delicately in her hands and felt an ache return as she glanced towards the others in her drawer. There was no variation between them besides white, beige, and black. They had no uniqueness, no style, and no lace. Instead, they were all that same cold and distant imitation satin. They were supposed to make her feel sexy, but they only reminded her that she was not normal.

But not Pinky, not the magical bra which gave her a sense of pride in its extra strength underwire and warm cotton embrace. The whole shape amazed her in its exquisite simplicity. Never before this bra had the straps been so thin, instead they were monster claws dug deeply into her shoulders. These thin straps had an adjustable gold strap that asked her what she wanted every time she slipped her arms in. Her other straps merely had three move, too loose-too tight-never right. But she could see the gold fading while the other bras remained so unchanged in the drawer. The moment she realized this, those lonely bras in the drawer were inviting her back to familiarity, right back to the old.

She knew it would be the same all over again, feeling so detached from her own body and she drew in a deep breath, refusing to give up on Pinky.

Her fingers carefully moved the gold clasps to their tightest form, ignoring the faint frizz they left upon the material as they moved. Then there was her now crooked underwire, which she fixed with a gentle tug of war motion between her hands. Her favorite feature of her mystic undergarment was beginning to wear like the others, and she could still see it so perfectly in the catalog. The first time she had seen or heard of such a thing was in that little booklet her friend had snuck into her house. Her mother had worn the same type of bra for years, passing the tradition down to her, so the very idea of underwire seemed dirty to her.

"Why not just serve them up on a platter, Nita?"

But that wire was anything but nasty. That full shape outlining her breasts with a proud W, reminding her she was a woman. She was not a freak. She was not some kind of genetic mutation. Instead, she possessed beauty and femininity just like her girls had prayed for.

"Wear them proudly! Booty, hips, and boobs are all some of God's greatest weapon known as woman!"

She smiled adoringly at Pinky, the only one who understood her. The only one who saw she just wanted to be normal, accepted. It understood her need for balance in the background layer of plain Jane pink and its second layer of intricate pattern lace. The plain cotton whispered to her, reminding her she was a treasure. She was not easy as the boys claimed shortly after she started developing at nine-years-old. It knew the realness of her body and that was no tissue or silicone to be found within its walls. Pinky's lace was the song just beyond that angel's affirmation. Its pattern took the shape of various sunflowers. When she stared long enough, she could see the butterflies fluttering in between the flowers. It reminded her she was alive, she was perfect in imperfection and she was free.

That's why Pinky had to remain a secret. It had to be bought in secret, slipped into the house, and in between the mattress and bedspring of her mattress. It wasn't for Mama to know. To her, girls were not supposed to feel sexy. They were not supposed to want frilly little panties and lacy bras. But when was the last time she had truly felt like a woman in that everyday armor? The last time she found courage in the sea of black, white, and beige? She knew Mama found nothing there, and that's why she had to get Pinky.

If it meant secretly washing the piece whenever Mama went to wash the 'others' down at the laundry mat so be it. If it meant lying on her bedroom floor, holding it up to the ceiling and drying it with only her gaze, she would consider it a privilege. It was her best friend. Her savior…a little reminder that everything would work out just fine. It would work out whether she rejected another guy or not; because something appreciated her body as is with no strings attached, no defilement necessary, just a close calm hug. It wanted to do nothing more than support her.

Knowing that feeling could come only from Pinky, she slipped it onto her body slowly and enjoyed the brush the straps gave her skin as they made their way up onto her shoulders. Standing before her full length bedroom mirror, she began to do the front clasps (yet another thing good girls were to know nothing about). She smoothed it against her chest and grinned slightly at the way the pink contrasted her caramel skin. Suddenly, she was there again. In that place of pure bliss, where she was normal and beautiful. The place where no one could touch her.

Nothing Worth Fighting For

A lot of people judge me and my actions, but the truth is I was very aware of what I was doing. I was not ashamed. Because my motivations were never secretive; I understood my place. I never wanted him to leave his wife. I understood he loved her, loved her family, and I was not suppose to factor into his life at all. I was comfortable with that, happy to live life as a phone call with no strings attached.

I don't want him. Not like that. Sure, he's gorgeous in every way. Maybe if I was less selfish, more motivated to share my life, I wouldn't be in the situation I'm in now.

The tap of my heel against the floor is annoying my neighbors at the next table; hell, it's annoying me.

I can't help it. I hate things like this. Those once in a lifetime conversations where you have everything planned mentally, hoping it doesn't go to shit the second somebody opens an old wound by saying the wrong thing.

Sitting here, waiting for him to show up for what I hope is our final meeting, I have to figure out a way to make him believe there is nothing between us.

Another nervous smile to the neighbor, I got to stop tapping my foot.

I wish I could tell you how it started. We met, the chemistry was crazy, and before I knew it I was waking up beside a married man. He and I had never done this before and the intention was to never let it happen again.

That was only three months ago.

Three months ago when I met him by chance through a friend. Then I met him alone for coffee. After that...it's blur. All I know is he looked at me once, and all I could see was sincerity in his blue eyes. He seemed almost pure in his innocent ideas about the world and how things should be. I wanted to taste that, desperately, but I never once wanted to possess it. I had to much respect for him to ever think that he could be mine.

I still want to know how any idiot could decide his life was so dispensable because of a couple weekends together? He's not that man. He's good.

And me? Believe me when I say, my life is not available to anyone. Out of everyone, I thought he understood.

Then, as unexpected as every time before, he was entering the restaurant.

My foot finally stopped tapping, and time paused long enough for me to stare.

It's hard not to spot a man so attractive from miles away. Short trimmed dark hair, piercing blue gaze, and the perfect amount of muscle beneath casual clothes. He straightened the light black jacket over his graphic t-shirt and dug into his slightly baggy jeans for his cell phone.

Before he could dial my number, I waved him over with a small smile. When I received his sexy grin in response, I nearly ran out.

He made his way over to the table, and my heart was pounding out of control. I was on the verge of an anxiety attack, recalling each time we had spent together without one ounce of shame.

"Hey," He took the seat across from me, attempting to place his hand on mine and retracting the moment I pulled away, "you haven't thought about what I had to say."

"I did. My mind hasn't changed."

"And why's that? You think I'm going to stay in my marriage because you say no?"

"I want nothing to do with whatever your decision is." I met his eyes with mine, trying to remain unaffected by the obvious disappointment in his eyes, "I want you to know that I will not be waiting for you when and if you leave your wife."

"Fine, it doesn't change the way I feel about anything." He reached across the table, catching my hand this time, and nearly melting me with his gaze, "Especially you."

"I don't want to be with you, Kevin."

An angry laugh left his lips as he released my hand, insisting, "You're scared."

"I'm not scared of anything, but you seem to be having a hard time with the truth."

"Do you actually think telling me now that you don't want anything to do with me is going to change what we've already done?"

"No."

"Then why not see where this goes? Why not give me a chance?"

"Because there's nothing to see. We have separate lives, and that's why this has worked this long. I have my things my life, and you have nothing to do with it. My money, my friends, and it's all my business. You were a happy accident, nothing more."

The taste of alcohol had never been more satisfying than in that moment when I finished off the worst cocktail of my life.

"I didn't have hour long conversations with myself, Jennifer. You were there, with me, for everything."

"You're mistaking fun for something else entirely, and I'm trying to tell you to stop. Don't turn your back on your life. You've got it good."

"I don't want to lose you."

"You don't have a choice."

Just as I was about to leave, his hand had caught my wrist and prevented me from doing so. He set those commanding eyes on me, signaling for me to sit, and I gave in, seeing as I had such a hard time resisting his stare.

You can say what you want about a man, look at whatever you want on him or question every personality trait he has, but the eyes say it all. Unfortunately, when a man knows his look is all it takes, a woman finds it hard to escape.

"If my marriage was perfect, you and I would have never happened. But it did, and I know what's what now."

"No, that's just what cheaters tell themselves so that they could sleep at night."

"And you tell yourself what at night?"

It was true. It stung. But I refused to let it show, responding, "I tell myself I have nothing to do with your getting a divorce because I don't want you to."

"I'm not turning my back on my family. I'll be there for my kids, but I don't want to be with my wife anymore."

"You're telling me you don't love her?"

"No, I will always love her but wanting a life with her is done and over with."

I was getting frustrated, tired of the fact that he still was not listening to a word I had to say.

"I told you all this, the last time we saw each other."

I had to laugh at the statement, very aware of the last time we had seen each other and what he said, "Because that's what I wanted for my birthday, a big box of guilt."

He leaned back, clearly growing weary of my failure to listen, "So, just forget you, right? Forget everything that's happened?"

"Nothing's happened. We slept together. It was fun. It's over. Don't go believing in the happy ending because there isn't one. Just go back to your home, and act like this was all a ***really*** good dream."

I headed out the door as fast as my heels would allow me, praying that God would allow me a graceful escape in such a scandalous deed. I was about to get in my car, when I felt his strong hand place a gentle touch on my shoulder. Shutting my eyes tightly, I fought myself to deny that surge of energy between us.

You can say whatever you want about me, but I find it hard to believe anyone could ignore the spark. It is something beyond all reason, beyond emotion, and it is electrifying to a point that you believe God has created this person just to bring something out of you. One touch and your whole body is shivering.

I released a deep breath, turning to face him, and stumbled once more into his stare, feeling all my motivations were fading into the very distant background.

"If you need time, that's all right. I'm getting the divorce. It has nothing and everything to do with you."

Those eyes were doing something to me, something I hated myself for.

The roughness of his palm softly caressed my cheek as he vowed, "I'm going to show you that we're not a mistake."

Bowing my head, I pulled his hand away yet held his hand for a moment to proclaim with the last of my strength, "There is no we."

With that, I managed to get into my car and drive away with only one glance into my rearview mirror.

La Niña Perdida

"Ma'am? Ma'am, I need you to stay on the line with me."

Rather than respond she allowed the phone to crash to the ground, it snapped shut from the impact. Her wide ebony eyes finally managed a blink and cleared her sight for the vision before her. Blood stained the white counter tops, the brown cabinets, and lead her straight to the black metal set upon the counter. Without a moment to react, the sickness had escaped the pit of her stomach and sent her to the kitchen sink beside her. She gagged and coughed until the very last of any food she had consumed had escaped her. The tears were already there, magnified only by the motion of her body, as she tried to comprehend what she had done. She allowed the sink to hold her weight, reaching only for the knob, and using her opposite hand to bring some of the coolest water to her heated face. When she had managed a clear and smooth breath, she pushed herself slowly off the counter and circled around to face the ultimate consequence.

He wrinkled his brow as she avoided his eyes, still shaking slightly, "Where'd you get the gun, Vero?"

She said nothing, holding the back of her hand to her puffy lips.

"Answer me!" He took a step towards her, immediately noticing she moved not an inch. Pausing for a moment, he registered once more where the gun was. He drew in a deep breath, holding his hands up in surrender, "All right, let's just—we'll talk. We'll figure it out."

As he finished the sentence, it was evident not one twitch of change had happened to her stance. Her eyes remained fixed towards something on the ground.

The anger was beginning to boil once more as his jaw tightened, "I suggest you say something and say it quickly."

Her hand slowly fell to her side, revealing her dropped jaw and the tears beginning to trickle down her cheeks. But it was different, unfamiliar. Her tears were not of desperation, of sorrow, or even fear. They were renewed, almost relieved. These lead him to follow her gaze towards the kitchen floor.

He stumbled backwards, out of breath, "What the f—"

There he was. Or some of him.

She stared at him, frozen in her spot, and tried to comprehend the past few minutes. But nothing made sense. Nothing was clear.

All that she could see was the shots she had planted in his chest. The blood had changed the color of his blue uniform, accompanied only by the car grease which had followed him home. But her hands quickly left those wounds and found the blood on his fists, the very last bit he had managed to get from her.

The very last.

"You—" He could find no words, looking at his own body, and shot a glare at her over his shoulder, "You shot me?"

She grabbed the gun once more off the counter and tightened her jaw to its strongest capacity.

"I heard a loud sound, Vero, but I didn't feel a thing. I didn't feel it." He took a few steps away from his body, from her, and tried to piece it together, "How could I not feel it?"

Kneeling slowly by his lifeless side, she kept the gun ready in front of her and eventually pressed to his temple.

He watched this, absolutely helpless, and followed her gaze towards the blood pooling at the corner of his mouth, causing a sob to travel up and out of her throat.

"That's right! Did it hit you?!" Unable to control himself, he allowed the words to erupt from the pit of his stomach, "You did this to me!"

She stared at him with a wounded gaze as he lay completely still. In that split second, he had come back to her. Seeming almost peaceful in his state, he was that man who saved her years ago. That angelic tan face could only belong to her Trey. The prominent scar on his left eyebrow the only indication the street had ever laid a hand on him. His brown waves soft and out of place. From the neck up, she could swear he was soundly asleep.

"*Bitch.*"

Trey saw the flash of something else in her eyes, undetectable, "What?"

She seemed different, again like she wasn't there, just as when he heard the loud bang.

"Vero, what are you going to do?"

She surveyed his broad figure and caught another glimpse of the bullet holes. She had to assure herself he would not come back. He couldn't. He had to pay for this. He had to pay for everything. It was his time.

"Tell me what's going on!"

Spotting the box peeking out of his breast pocket, she slowly reached in and retrieved the last stick of relief. Glancing at his pale face, holding the cigarette in one hand and reaching back for his lighter with the other, she rose a brow, "Mind?"

Trey was in total disbelief, "You're crazy!"

Her angel remained still, the monster finally sleeping within him. She leaned back against the kitchen islander behind her and lit the cigarette with calm hands, taking a drag the moment she spotted the reddish glow at its tip. It was sweet relief, like a breath of fresh air among the sights suffocating her in the room.

"I gotta think." Trey ran his hands into his short hair, pacing back and forth, and felt the adrenaline begin to surge, "There's a way out of this. There always is. I just have to think, figure it out, and it'll come. It'll just appear."

"You promised."

Her soft cry stopped his tracks, causing his attention to redirect towards her.

"I believed you. I believed every word. I never thought twice, not even this time, and—you were suppose to do me right, Trey. You were suppose to make it right."

"Don't you think I wanted to!" He grinded his palms into his temples, closing his eyes in full awareness of the 'incident', "I didn't want to lose the kid, Vero! I didn't know, I wasn't thinking, and the next thing I knew…you were just laying there."

"You took her from me."

"I wanted her! I wanted you!" He dropped his hands, balling them quickly into stone fists, yet stopped short when reminded of his predicament, "I messed up. I was going to fix it. But you did this." Gesturing towards his body, he let out a soft and angry laugh, "Now, I can't do anything."

"It was suppose to be different this time. And now look…" When she saw he was finally listening, not a bit of response, she lost it with a scream, "Look!!!"

Pounding the back of her hand lightly against her forehead, she ignored the ash build up at the end of her cigarette and shut her eyes tightly, "Chella said it would happen. She said if I left. But you were the one who stopped my father and I was so sure…"

She took another drag, savoring his face. The smoothness of his skin among those strong cheekbones and even on his slightly pointed nose. His slightly pouty lips which had removed so many wounds, had made so many promises, and taken over her whole life—whatever it was.

"Do you remember the fair?" She softened her voice, crossing her legs, and tried to speak among her quivering lip, "When—when you said we'd have the life? The one with a big house, a big family, and everything we had never had."

Rather than look at her, reminded of what he had done again in her swollen face, he whispered, "I meant it."

Leaning over to his face, she allowed the warm of her breath to blow against the chill of his face, "You said you'd protect us. You said you'd protect me."

"I did. Not one thing came at you ever." *Except me*. The words had almost made it into the sentence, but he could find no courage to verbalize them, "I wanted to give you everything."

Shaking her head slowly, she searched his expression for a change and grew angry when there was none, "I would have given that to you. All of me, you had it."

"I didn't deserve it, Vero." A mist in his eyes, he glanced up at her, "You never got that. You never got that I didn't deserve any of it."

Silence, not even the tick of a clock to remind her time was moving, until she growled, "But you ruined it. Everything."

"I had to. I had to before you took it away." He fell to his knees, snickering at his body, "I had to win."

She moved in closer, hissing against him, "You ruined it when you took my baby."

"I'll make it up to you. I'll make this right."

Pushing away his voice once again, she erupted in the lowest of manners – needing him to hear every word, "I didn't care about anything. Not the yelling, cheating, none of that shit."

"I know."

"Did I leave when you hit me?"

"No."

"Not once, I stood by you. I was loyal to you. The only thing I ever asked you for was her!"

"I know." He swallowed a lump in his throat, drifting his eyes up once more to find her.

Breaking into uncontrollable tears, she fell back against the islander once more. Her arms slowly circled around her slim figure, another reminder her that there was no longer the bump. That little lump under her shirt was gone. The one she had built her hopes upon; the one she needed to go on; the one she needed to stay with him.

"You weren't allowed to have her!!!"

Trey stayed seated, taken aback yet again by her defense, taken back by her anger towards him.

She stopped after the words had left her lungs, needing air to return before trying to continue, "...did you even think about it, T? Did you even—" She tried to speak through tears, pleading with the limp body for her, "Didn't you think about the baby...about our baby. Why couldn't you just wait?"

"I don't know! I don't know why it happened! I don't know why I keep messing up! I just do, Vero!"

She hit her head against the solid surface behind her, "Tell me you saw her. That—you heard her laugh—that you heard her cry or call out for her daddy."

"Stop it."

The light touch of an ash brushed her knuckles, causing her to look at the half lit stick, and returned her eyes to his stone expression, "Tell me you're sorry for taking her away."

Ashamed, he responded, "I am."

She was at his face again. The moment she felt compelled to make up his words, give him an excuse, she brought the burning cigarette to his cheek and settled it into the skin with an angry frown, whispering, "Unforgivable."

Her action reignited the fire within him, causing him to spring to his feet, "You're not innocent, Vero! You could have left whenever you wanted! Nothing, not a damn thing, kept you with me except you!" Taking one large step to her side, he leaned into her face, "You made promises too. You were suppose to be there, and I knew you'd leave! All along, you lied! You said you would be the one who stayed, who made things easier, only to betray me like this!"

Leaning back, they heard the loud pounding on the door.

She managed to catch vague indication of the police yet stayed seated while tossing the cigarette aside.

Trey slowly found his way to a stand, spotting the cops entering from his peripheral. As they made their ways towards him, her eyes found their way upward and into his.

The words softly, coldly left her lips to proclaim, "You can't take anything else from me."

"You see me?" He could not get an answer from her before the cops were helping her to her feet, "Vero, answer me!"

The cops seemed all too understanding while loosely fitting the handcuffs to her wrists.

"You can't leave me like this. You have to do something!" Trey's pleas went completely ignored as the cops walked her right through him, "Vero, help me!" They walked her out the door as he screamed, "You can't leave me here like this! Vero!!!"

One of the cops closed the door, leaving him in a silent room with nothing but his dead body and what he had done to her.

Ladies of a New World

He's a liar. Always has been. But I had to get hurt before I realized it. I couldn't get it in all my girls telling me. Or in Mama's warning. Or even in my brother's hateful eyes. Nope. Had to have my heart broken over and over until I lost count. Until he ran out of second chances. But even now, clutching my bitterness, my anger, and self righteous attitude that I am flawless, I hope for him. Hope that it isn't true, and somewhere somehow he told the truth. Isn't that pathetic? I'm supposed to be independent, a true woman of the new world. Buying my things, telling fools off, and reminding myself that it is a crime to be this fine!

Instead, I sit here in an empty apartment, curled on the couch with a blanket that's God knows how old. I find myself waiting for a phone that never rings and a door that has yet to be pounded on. But I can't be weak. I'm not allowed. Dad's dead and my brother's already a failure. I have to make something of myself and save us all from mediocrity. Hope and a broken heart are just two more luxuries that I just can't afford. I better get back in my room before Mama finds me. The last thing I need is a lecture about being strong, about being the woman in this family who 'makes it'.

Ugh, my room's a mess. Who would have known that packing would make things more chaotic in this tiny room. I didn't even think I had this many clothes. And, look, there it is. A picture of me and him, sitting on that pile of clothes, just begging to be tucked away with all my crap. It's back when we were happy, when I didn't know he was a liar or cheater.

Isn't it a wonder how pictures always stay smooth, despite throwing them or moving them in and out of a frame? They always manage to remind of you when things were absolutely perfect and nothing could go wrong. I wonder if I burn it, will the image stay this perfect in my mind? And that smile, how could one man's smile be so deceiving to a welcoming woman's heart? I was never supposed to trust a man anyway. They always leave you. Mama says whether by choice or not, they'll always leave you to carry the home, which is why I have to take care of myself. I've got to let his smile and lies go. I've got to show the women to come in our family that one of us made. One of us did not let a man, a baby, or anything else stop us.

I better finish packing. I've got a flight early morning, then I get to leave him behind.

I wonder if I should bring my blanket with me. It's kind of ratty, but—it would be nice.

Maybe the other two girls I'm moving in with will have teddy bears or bibles. They seemed descent enough on the phone. They're both like me, waiting to fly out to Cali and change it all around. Nina, Mia, and 'Shorty'. What a threesome, huh? It all started with a small online advertisement, a home for rent to three responsible students. Let's hope that little expensive place can contain all of us. Big families make big noise, and we're all ready for the change.

I'm praying that includes at least one study hour before we're craving a home cooked meal, loud salsa music, and families back home. Because we've all got a job to do. We've all got to succeed.

~*~

You see her across the room. She seems so calm and composed, flipping casually through a gossip magazine as you contemplate the biggest decision of your life. It's today or never. You must choose— its life or your own. God forbid you imagine it as a he or she because that will make it to real. Who knew that one last goodbye with your novio would end like this.

You know Ricky can't handle this. If you do this, however you do it, you do it alone.

Your big hazel eyes wonder towards the door, life is waiting for you out there. A nice little apartment in Cali, away from New Mexico with two other Latinas. All of you the promise of a family. And, after one little procedure, you could still have it. It would be right back in your hands. You can walk out and follow the sun all the way to UCLA. Your roommates are waiting for you, they could be your lifelong friends, and you'd be the first.

Mia, that is all you've ever wanted—to just be first. The first with a career that didn't mean taking orders or cleaning some other woman's big beautiful house. All you have to do is wait for them to call your name. And be assured, no one knows you're here. No one from your neighborhood would venture to this side of town, it's too stuck up. They wouldn't be able to stand some of the very eyes that looked down upon you as you entered this place.

You try to absorb all the smiling women on the walls, each one promising you that there is a life after this. Each one assuring you that you somehow have a choice in all this. That you are responsible for your own path and what comes with it, including diapers and breast feedings.

But you find it hard to believe. Even now, you've checked in and everything—yet you're sure this is unreal. It can't happen. Because your life has always been about everyone but you, and why is now any different? When the family needed your help at the restaurant, you were the one to step in. When Mom needed you to help care for the new baby, you were the one who did it. When Ricky needed just one more night with you, one more night to love you, you let him. And it was never about you.

You readjust in the barely cushioned plastic and know that it can finally be about you. This is your shot, and you're taking it. You have to make it about you, or its life will be as hard as your own. Its life will be ruined. You close your eyes, the tears suddenly make you realized how cold your stare had become. What if it was going to look like Ricky? Big brown eyes, a smile that took up its whole face, and a laugh that just made you melt. What if it wanted to be with Mama all the time, grew up just to make you happy? Did you ever think that maybe this choice meant more love and happiness than anywhere outside of this office?

"Mia Vasquez."

You hear them call your name, but you remain glued to your seat. Suddenly, you can't forget your little brother's hugs or your niece's giggle. You can't forget your whole family, everyone's love and support for you as well as everything you do. You'll work it out.

If it means quitting school after a semester or giving the baby to someone else, you've got to let it—he or she—have a choice.

~*~

Shorty stood intimidated in front of the church door, convincing herself this was the last stop before her flight, and swallowed whatever doubt was caught in her throat. Inhaling as much air as her lungs would allow, she pushed all of her tiny frame into the heavy brown wood and entered the church of her upbringing.

Upon entrance, she immediately bowed her head. Her index and middle finger immediately creating the symbol of the cross against her body. Shorty quickly felt ashamed, dressed so casually in a Catholic church was anything but appropriate. Jeans, sneaks, and a tank top were far from the last subdued dress she had worn here. But that was ages ago. It was before she knew. It was before the excuses. It was before the shame and judgment.

Releasing the same deep breath from moments ago, she thanked whoever was listening for the solitude and slid onto a pew. Shorty nervously wrung her hands in her lap and stared towards the front of the church, her eyes quickly set upon a sunlit crucifix. Jesus was helpless and hopeful as his form stood against it, shaded only but stained glass window. It felt as if he could not look at her, his head facing towards the sky and she felt again. This was no longer the place for her. This was no longer home.

She could not help but release a soft sob, "I'm so sorry."

She knew it was wrong. Her life. Her choice. Her love. It was all wrong, and her choice would mean losing it all. Shorty knew that she could hide it from everyone except her religion. The Saints, Jesus, and God all knew her deep dark secret. They all knew her hidden life. They all knew that school, living away from NY, was just another excuse to continue living this way.

But it ran too deep. Her heart and her mind were operating in unison, only since she had let go. Let of her life of before. She found the strength to stare upon the cross once more, begging for some forgiveness. Begging for understanding. Begging God to make it better, to understand she had tried. She had tried to date men, horrible men and gentlemen, but they were never right for her. Not one made her feel this way, none were like Neveah. Reaching into her deep baggy jean pocket, she found her last given from Nevaeh tight within her grasp. The only person, the only soul, who understood her. She smiled sadly to herself, using her free hand to wipe tears, and took in the sight of a rainbow colored cross. For a moment, in that pew, she did not feel out of place.

Shorty took the chain and put it around her neck then proceeded to slide down to her knees. Bowing her head, she clasped her hands around the cross and stared towards Jesus one last time. Through a teary gaze, she thought of herself and her new life. As calmly as she could, she shakily recited the prayer, "Angel of God, my guardian dear, to whom God's love commits me here. Ever this day be at my side, to enlight and guard, to rule and guide."